Praise for *Sm*

"In each of Nicola Winstanley's powerful stories we feel for and feel tender toward, even love, these characters trying to navigate through their lives the best they can, with earnest hope and often unrecognized resilience as they find ways to make do and, despite everything, continue to be themselves, to find agency and possibility. *Smoke* leaves the reader looking into the future, wondering what will become of these people, what will become of all of us, recognizing how lives are often betrayed by the way the world is – often because of the brokenness of men – but also buoyed by the very humanness, the fragility and strength of the women. *Smoke* isn't a sugar pill, but something far more effective: a clear-eyed and compassionate tonic for strength and courage." – Gary Barwin, author of *Imagining Imagining* and *Yiddish for Pirates*

"In *Smoke*, Nicola Winstanley gives us a recurring cast of characters who we follow over their transition from girlhood to womanhood, growing up too fast in a world that has all but given up on them. But Winstanley also gives her characters hope, writing with raw, honest, unsentimental prose that infuses her stories with insight and humanity that shines a beacon of light through the bleak landscape of their lives. Nicola Winstanley is a fresh new voice in short fiction, and I'll be thinking about these stories for a long time." – Amy Jones, author of *Pebble & Dove* and *We're All in This Together*

"'A bad thing happens and then it never stops,' says one of the characters in Nicola Winstanley's empathetic and compelling collection. This is a beautiful book that gnaws at your heart with its stories about the pervasiveness of intergenerational trauma and the persistent human need to search for love, stability and connection." – Meaghan Strimas, author of *Yes or Nope* and *A Good Time Had by All*

"Winstanley's stories move effortlessly between dark and light, between innocence lost and joy gained. She writes characters with a brutal kind of beauty, imbued with sorrow and longing that force us to face things we'd like to ignore, but can't because their universal truths reside in all of us. These are intimate, sharp, incandescent stories that assuredly declare that while suffering is an inevitable part of our lives, we can choose to not let it define us. A raw, funny and heartbreaking debut." – John Vigna, author of *No Man's Land* and *Bull Head*

"The stories in Nicola Winstanley's meticulously crafted and emotionally walloping debut behave like smoke itself: spreading slowly, getting into every corner, twisting and thickening and darkening, all while the characters that inhabit them struggle to put out the fires that threaten to engulf them. This is a collection that builds in power and strength: by the time you reach its final, unexpectedly grace-filled moments, you are blinking away tears." – Nathan Whitlock, author of *Lump* and *Congratulations on Everything*

SMOKE

Also by Nicola Winstanley

Children's Picture Books
A Bedtime Yarn
Cinnamon Baby
How to Give Your Cat a Bath in Five Easy Steps
How to Teach Your Cat a Trick in Five Easy Steps
Mel and Mo's Marvellous Balancing Act
The Pirate's Bed

SMOKE

NICOLA WINSTANLEY

A Buckrider Book

Published by Buckrider Books
an imprint of Wolsak and Wynn Publishers
280 James Street North
Hamilton, ON L8R2L3
www.wolsakandwynn.ca

Editor for Buckrider Books: Paul Vermeersch | Editor: Jen Hale
Copy editor: Jamila Allidina
Cover and interior design: Jen Rawlinson
Author photograph: Chris Palmer
Typeset in Adobe Caslon Pro and Proxima Nova
Printed by Brant Service Press Ltd., Brantford, Canada

10 9 8 7 6 5 4 3 2 1

The publisher gratefully acknowledges the support of the Canada Council for the Arts and the Ontario Arts Council. We also acknowledge the financial support of the Government of Canada through the Canada Book Fund and the Government of Ontario through the Ontario Book Publishing Tax Credit and Ontario Creates.

Library and Archives Canada Cataloguing in Publication

Title: Smoke / Nicola Winstanley.
Names: Winstanley, Nicola, author.
Identifiers: Canadiana 20240356594 | ISBN 9781989496893 (softcover)
Subjects: LCGFT: Short stories.
Classification: LCC PS8645.I57278 S66 2024 | DDC C813/.6—dc23

For Walter

CONTENTS

Smoke /1

Everything Happens for a Reason /19

Amanda's Baptism /37

Chicken /61

Rubber /79

Breach /93

It Means "Beloved" /109

Feeling in the Flesh /133

Keys /149

Will You Be a Christian? /167

Purify /187

Acknowledgements /205

SMOKE

At six o'clock, all the mothers singsong "Dinnertime!" into the echoing valley, and the kids in the playground jump down from swings and slides and run barefoot across the prickle-sharp grass and up the long driveway to the street where they live side by side in wooden bungalows surrounded by shaved, green lawns.

"Clare!"

"Hurry, Fiona!" her mother calls, because Fiona huffs when she runs and comes last to the table every single night.

"Dinner, Kenneth! I said, *dinner*!"

Kenneth tosses a tennis ball high into the air and still three more times after his mother's final "Kenneth, I mean it!"

"Clare, darling!"

Clare yanks the other end of the skipping rope from Amanda's hand, loops it neatly, then crouches to buckle her patent-leather sandals.

Amanda is already at the bottom of the driveway by the time Clare catches up to her. "It's not fair," Clare says. "You don't even have to go."

Amanda stops suddenly. For the last few weeks, she had been going home at dinnertime, same as everyone else, as if her mother's voice rang out too. But no one called her now. She just hadn't noticed yet.

"You don't even have a mother." Clare pokes Amanda in the chest with her finger. "You get to stay here and do whatever you want." Then she runs up the hill and doesn't say bye to Amanda or look back once.

"See ya later," Amanda whispers. "Have a nice dinner."

When all the other kids have gone, Amanda sits on a swing and kicks at the dry dirt beneath. Dust puffs and settles on her skinned knees. They had been playing horses, and, as usual, Amanda was the horse, on all fours. Clare had bridled her with the skipping rope and guided her to the gravel. When Amanda hesitated, Clare had said, "Horses who misbehave get cropped," and threatened to use the belt from the waistband of her corduroys.

Amanda licks her palm and rubs at the dirt and grazes on her knees; it stings.

On the ridge, behind the cabbage trees and Norfolk pines, the Auckland sun is melting like a pink marshmallow. School has started, but it seems like summer still, warm with a little breeze and the lazy buzzing of fat flies. On the other side of Mr. Grayson's six-foot fence, Clive barks hard at nothing, then stops. His chain clunks as he lies down again in his doghouse. Amanda pumps her bare legs listlessly, stretches out until she is nearly horizontal. She floats above the ground, her hair trailing, while the swing tilts up and back, its hinge screeching like a slow, far-off train whistle.

Soon, the sun is just a blinking eye on the horizon, and Amanda climbs the ladder on the tall slide to get a better view of the houses all around. The kids are at their dinner tables now, saying grace. Soon their fathers will come home, and their mothers will put the kids to bed and tuck them in with goodnight kisses. The mummies will say, "Sleep tight, don't let the bedbugs bite," and leave the bedroom doors ajar so it isn't too dark. Then the kids will close their eyes and go to sleep.

Amanda had waited in the hospital corridor with Judy while their father was in their mother's room. When he came out, he closed the door behind him and said, "She's gone." Amanda thought her mother had taken a holiday without telling them. Then her father had started to cry.

Amanda still wasn't sure where her mother had gone or when she would be coming back. She hadn't been allowed to go to the funeral.

The outlines of the play equipment begin to dissolve in the spreading dark. "Clive," Amanda yells. "Clive, ya dumb mutt!"

Not even a rattle from his doghouse.

By the time Amanda runs home, the darkness rises from the ground like smoke. Streetlights hum, then flicker on.

Judy is reading on the sofa. "Where have you been? It's too late to be out. You're naughty."

"What's for dinner?"

"I'm telling." Judy wraps one mousy ringlet around her finger and twists. "There's only toast again, and you can make it yourself." Her eyes slide back to her book.

"What are you reading?" Judy stares at the page, sniffs and wipes her nose with the back of her hand. "Judy?"

They have a new kind of toaster – the kind that pops the toast. Amanda likes the way the toast jumps and the sound it makes. Their father, Ernie, bought it after the funeral, and also an electric kettle and an automatic washing machine. Judy doesn't know how to use the washing machine, but they're the only people on the street who don't have a wringer-washer now. When Clare's mum, Mrs. Price, came to see it after the social workers had left, she said, "What a pigsty!" as soon as she stepped into the house. She told Ernie that he would have to give her six dollars a week and she would do the laundry and the hoovering on Wednesdays. "And make your own bed, young lady," she said to Amanda on the way out. But the house always looked like it had been hit by a tornado by Friday night, and Amanda hadn't made her bed once.

"Amanda!" Judy yells from the lounge. "Don't you have a

nose?" Grey smoke pours from the toaster slots. "Don't waste the bread. And you have to open a window so we don't suffocate, for goodness's sake!"

Amanda has to get the toast out with a fork and scrape the black off before buttering it and sprinkling on the sugar, but it doesn't really matter; she likes the burned taste. Sometimes Ernie forgets to give Judy money so she can buy bread at the dairy after school, and then there's only stale bread and the toast is dry and hard, and sometimes the butter is rancid or there are ants in the sugar – but not today.

Amanda squishes on the sofa beside Judy. She takes huge bites of toast and chews with her mouth open, satisfied with the clack-clack it makes.

"Stop it," Judy says. "I can't read if you're going to eat like that."

"There was no lunch!" Amanda licks at the sweet butter that ticklish-drips down her wrist until Judy snaps her book shut.

At half past nine, Ernie appears and drops his briefcase on the floor. He hesitates. "What's that doing there?" he says, finally, and points to a carving knife lying on the velour recliner seat. He pulls on his tie to loosen it, yanks it over his head and throws it beside the knife.

"Amanda was late home."

"What?" Ernie pinches the skin between his eyebrows, above his new glasses. His eyebrows are black and thick, and his eyelashes curl as pretty as a girl's, but Amanda is never to say that again, ever. "I've had a long day." He disappears into the kitchen.

"Well?" Judy yells over the sound of running water. "She didn't come home for dinner!"

"Some dinner." Amanda pokes Judy's upper arm. "You're not Mum."

"I know that, but I'm supposed to look after you."

"I can do what I want. You can't stop me."

Ernie is back, hovering. "Can't I have some peace and quiet?"

"Go ahead!" Judy slams the door on her way out.

Amanda has won the argument, but it doesn't feel like it.

Ernie changes the channel on the TV set to the ten o'clock news, turns the sound up loud, then sits on a hard-backed kitchen chair, a mug of tea balanced on his knee. Petrol prices are going up. Ernie groans and shifts uncomfortably, straightens out his leg with the missing kneecap. When the business report comes on at half past ten, Amanda says, "Should I go to bed?" He looks at her and frowns, as though he doesn't know who she is.

In bed, she pulls a tangled blanket over the same clothes she wore all day and falls right to sleep.

The room is bright. It must be late. Then the thrum of a lawn mower and Amanda realizes: it's Saturday. Ernie will be home, and the weather is good. He will take her to tennis, or maybe the beach. She kicks her bedding onto the floor and sprints to the bathroom.

Ernie is there already, shaving. A towel wrapped around his waist, he leans over the sink, his face a few inches from the mirror, and draws the razor through the foam on his cheek. A smooth strip of tanned skin appears.

"I need to go to the toilet." A faint rasp, and another strip. "Dad!"

"You'll have to wait."

Amanda slides down the door frame and sits, squeezing her upper thighs together and trying not to think about it. But it's not so bad; she likes watching Ernie shave. After each stroke, he dips the razor into the sink and the soapy water gurgles and splashes along with the transistor radio on the window ledge singing, "American Top 40!"

When the Bee Gees come on the radio, Ernie makes a choking sound. "Why do they sing like that? They sound like women." He takes off his glasses, rinses his face with clean water and pats it dry with a raggedy towel. He can barely see without his glasses, and without them he looks like a different person, like a kid – as though he has another face you only get to see when he can't see you.

"I like them. Judy said she's going to teach me the Brooklyn Hustle. Why don't you use aftershave, like on TV?"

Ernie shakes his head. "Men don't wear perfume." He puts his glasses back on and tries to see the back of his head in the mirror, pulling at the short hair where it stops at the top of his neck. "My hair isn't too long, is it?"

"Can we go to the beach today?"

"I have to get dressed."

"Can Clare come? Can we get an ice cream?" Amanda calls after him, then sits on the toilet, at last. She hums along loudly to "How Deep Is Your Love" until it's the chorus, and then she sings the words.

Ernie is by the front door in a suit. "I'll be gone most of the day." Before Amanda even thinks to remind him that it's Saturday, the door clicks shut.

From her bedroom window, Amanda watches Ernie fling open the door of his car, get in and pull the door shut. No slamming! It's a company car, shiny dark green. Hunter green. He puts his briefcase on the passenger side, then adjusts the rear-view mirror, and maybe that's why he doesn't see what Amanda sees – Mrs. Price rushing down her driveway in an apron and fluffy slippers, then waving one arm over her head while she crosses the street – because Ernie starts the engine and begins to reverse. He doesn't seem to notice she's there until she bangs three times on the car boot with her open hand and he has to stop. She comes around and taps on Ernie's window, and he winds it down slowly. Her voice is loud and sharp, but Amanda can't make out the words. Ernie nods his head, staring straight ahead, until she stops talking, and then Ernie reverses out of the driveway with a jolt and a screech. Mrs. Price folds her arms and watches him speed away, then looks back toward Amanda's bedroom, frowning. Amanda ducks. She has probably done something wrong.

Judy's bed is empty and neatly made, her clothes all put away, not all over the floor like Amanda's. Judy's not in the kitchen either.

There's no bread left, so Amanda has Shrewsbury biscuits for breakfast, and instant coffee with four teaspoons of sugar. Judy says Amanda is too young for coffee, but she's not here.

Amanda wanders out to the street, where all the children play when they are not at the park. There is no sign now of Mrs. Price, but Clare flits around the spiral of a sprinkler on their front lawn, jumping over the arcing water as if it's a skipping rope. When Amanda waves and runs over, Clare jumps back from the spray, plants her hands on her hips, and looks up and down at Amanda's too-tight T-shirt and flared purple jeans, short by two inches. "That T-shirt was dirty yesterday." Clare is one year older than Amanda, and she is smooth and pale, and white-blond, and thin as a whip. She has long legs, longer than most other girls, her mother says so, and Amanda is nearly six inches shorter – they've measured. Amanda has baby fat and freckles and a gap between her front teeth. Clare's teeth stick out because she still sucks her thumb in secret, but she'll get braces as soon as she's old enough. "It's a good thing you do well in school," Mrs. Price says to Amanda whenever she sees the two girls playing together.

"I slept in this outfit," Amanda brags. "Do you want to come to my house and make fudge?" Clare is never allowed to use the stove at her house or eat things with sugar.

"Is Judy there to supervise?"

. . .

Amanda and Clare make fudge, extra careful with the boiling liquid sugar as they stir it on the stove, and when they pour it in the pan, because if it splashes it will burn enough to take their skin off. Then they sit behind the twelve-foot-high monkey-apple hedge that hides Amanda's house from the road and eat the fudge while they collect monkey apples off the ground. Later, they'll throw the apples at the boys who ride their banana bikes on the pavement, hooting and laughing, as if they own the whole street.

By half past twelve, Amanda and Clare have eaten most of the fudge and gathered two sand buckets full of the tiny apples, but that's right when Mrs. Price calls from the other side of the hedge, "Come home for lunch, Clare. It's no use hiding. I can see your sandals." Amanda stays put because when Clare appears from beneath the hedge, dress and face smeared with fudge and dirt, her mother scolds her. "What were you doing? I know Amanda's father wasn't there, young lady. Was Judy? Go home now." Then Mrs. Price crouches so she can see Amanda between the leaves. "Your father came home late last night. Past your bedtime," she says, as though it was Amanda's fault. "And he's out again today."

"No," Amanda lies. "He came home early then went out again, then came back. He has to work today."

Kenneth rides past and yells through the hedge, "Bullrush!" and Amanda turns from Mrs. Price and runs barefoot after him as fast as she can.

Amanda spends all day in the park with the other kids. They play bullrush and statues and soccer until four o'clock when the teenagers arrive. The teenage girls have low-cut T-shirts and cleavage, and they wear skin-tight jeans and feather earrings. The boys have long hair, and one of them carries a bright-red disco boom box on his shoulder. The other little kids scatter, but Amanda stays behind to watch the teenagers flirt and smoke. Fiona's sister Mimi pretends she doesn't know who Amanda is and doesn't look her way. Then a boy pushes her up against the pole of the swing set, and Mimi and the boy smush against each other and kiss like they do in the movies. Then the boy leans around Mimi and winks at Amanda.

"Hey, you want one?" He waves his cigarette in her direction.

"Don't," Mimi says, but he shakes a cigarette from a golden box of Benson & Hedges, lights it on the end of his own and offers it to Amanda. Amanda's mother smoked the same kind, two packs a day. Amanda takes the cigarette, puts it between the knuckles of her first and middle finger, then up to her lips. She drags and doesn't cough, blows the smoke out her mouth in an O. Amanda knows how to do it from sneaking puffs when her mother wasn't watching.

"Check it out!" The boy laughs and slaps his thigh.

The boy's friends come and watch her.

Amanda's head spins. She is hit by a wave of nausea and wants to spit on the ground. She has never felt more special in her whole life.

"Isn't it about time you went home?" Mimi says.

"Why? There's no one there." Amanda takes another drag and exhales. She stares at the smoke as it spirals in the cooling air, dissolves and disappears.

When it's nearly dark, the teenagers leave. "Go home, Amanda!" Mimi yells from the top of the driveway. The others laugh, as though it's funny. As their laughter fades, Amanda stands alone in the shadow of Mr. Grayson's fence and listens. Faint music. Cars far away. A door slammed shut. Her own breath. Then nothing. Her fingertips and lips tingle.

In the half-light, barely visible and all alone, she realizes she is boundless now, like smoke.

•   •   •

None of the lights are on at home, and it's nearly dark. Amanda flicks the switch in the hall, and the bulb splutters, fizzes and dies. The kitchen is grey and still. There's a note on the table from Judy that says she will be at Vivienne's and staying the night. No note from Ernie.

Amanda crawls behind the sofa and extracts from underneath it the fudge she hid in case Judy came home and found it. She sits down right there and chips at the dry lump with her teeth, taking her time. Each sliver melts slowly in her mouth. She stays crouched in the gap between the sofa and the wall gnawing on sugar and daydreaming until it's late and she is too tired to stay awake anymore, then she lies down on her side and falls asleep.

It takes Amanda a long time to remember where she is when she wakes up at dawn. Her neck is sore, her hip bruised. She runs her sticky hands down the sofa upholstery to clean them before wriggling from her spot.

The kitchen light is still on, and everything is where it was the night before. Her father's bedroom is exactly the same as the day before too – the pillows scattered, the bedspread in a puddle on the edge of the bed, the closet door open and a mess inside, laundry and papers thrown over the boxes full of her mother's things.

Amanda slides one of her father's old suit jackets off its hanger. The lining is slightly scratchy and cool on her arms. It smells of shaving cream and hair oil. Sunlight soap. Her father's smell. Musk and bitter lemon. The jacket comes all the way to her knees, and though it isn't cozy exactly, she wraps herself in it, then lies down on the bed and waits.

At last, Ernie's key clicks in the lock and Amanda jumps up to meet him at the door. "Where were you?"

It's not an accusation, but Ernie's jaw goes up and down

goldfish-like, as if he's been caught. "Why are you up so early? It's Sunday."

"You weren't here last night."

"I was. I went out early this morning for a run." He's wearing his work clothes from the morning before, but no tie.

"I don't care. I wasn't scared." Amanda flaps the too-long sleeves of the jacket, like a baby bird trying out its wings. "You can leave me here whenever you want. I'm old enough to look after myself."

"I saw you fast asleep in bed when I came home late, then got up early."

Amanda stops flapping and stares up at Ernie. His face is pale, fallen and unshaven. He smiles awkwardly, like an adult who doesn't know her and is trying to be nice. "Oh. Okay." The jacket slides from Amanda's narrow shoulders and onto the floor, and she wraps her bare arms around her chest to stop the feeling unfurling inside her. It creeps and burns. She didn't know before that adults could lie. But now she does. What else has he lied about? "If you say so." Ernie doesn't say anything about the jacket, and she doesn't bother to pick it up.

At school on Monday, Clare won't play with Amanda. "My mother says you have no supervision, and your father is a disgrace. She says you're running wild and a bad influence."

After that, the other kids won't play with Amanda either because Clare is the boss. Fiona won't sit with her, and Fiona is nobody's friend, just a tagalong, so Amanda is all alone through lunch, and lunch-less too because Ernie slept all Sunday afternoon and forgot about the groceries.

At the picnic table across the narrow playground, Clare sits up straight, opens her Tupperware and neatly stabs cheese cubes with a fork, staring at Amanda the whole time.

. . .

Later, Amanda realizes she has lost her bus ticket and has to walk home. It's better this way because she will not have to see Clare, who had kept glancing over her shoulder at Amanda all afternoon, as if Amanda were on her back somehow and had to be shaken off.

Kenneth nearly knocks her down with his bike, then brakes to a sudden stop, hops off and doubles back. "Your mum died, aye?"

Amanda shrugs. She doesn't want to think about it anymore.

"It was a dog? Whose dog?"

"It wasn't a dog."

"Yeah it was. Clare said that."

"She doesn't know anything."

"Then what?" But Amanda couldn't answer; she didn't know herself. "Sucks to have no mum." Kenneth sniffed.

"How would you know?"

"My mum left yesterday. Took her suitcase and that. You know?"

"Forever?"

"She might come back. But Dad said don't bother." He jumped back on his bike. "Anyways, see ya."

She might come back? Amanda is so happy she nearly runs home.

When Judy finally gets home, Amanda jumps up off the sofa. "I have something to tell you! Kenneth's mother left, but she –"

"I have to tell you something first." Judy takes a big bad-news breath and sits stiffly beside Amanda. "Vivienne's mother said I could stay with them for a while if I wanted to, in their spare room." She puts a hand on Amanda's shoulder, like an adult, even though she's only twelve.

There is a yellow-faced puppet on the TV singing "Happy day!

Let's play!" over and over. Amanda stares at the puppet and won't look at Judy. "I can have your room."

"Her mother thinks I need more stability because of school. Because I'll be going to high school soon." Judy stares at the side of Amanda's face; Amanda can see out of the corner of her eye. "Will you be all right if I'm not here?" Judy is always such a baby and almost crying about everything.

"You don't have to stay," Amanda says to the TV screen. She wants to say, "I don't need you," but it will hurt Judy's feelings too much and then Judy will cry for real. "How many weeks?" Amanda asks. The puppet's bright-pink, flat mouth opens and shuts.

"Maybe for the rest of the first term. At least."

"Oh."

"Stop watching TV!" Judy lunges forward and clicks off the set.

Amanda turns to Judy, free of the puppet's demands at last. "So? Can I have your room while you're gone?" Then Judy is mad, her lips pressed together – but she pretends she's not. "Well, you won't be needing it."

"Don't you care whether or not I live here?"

"You're never here anyway. What difference does it make?"

Judy moves out a few days later and takes all her records and her record player with her and all her clothes. She leaves the broderie anglaise bedspread Amanda coveted once, the last birthday present Judy got from their mother, and she says Amanda can sleep in her bed if she wants to.

Instead, Amanda starts sleeping in Ernie's bed, the side where her mother used to sleep. She sleeps with the light on until Ernie comes home, then she wakes up and pretends to be asleep, and he turns off the light and lies heavily on the bed facing her. He never says anything or moves her to her own bed, just falls asleep immediately. After a while, Amanda puts her face close to his to make sure he's breathing. She breathes in his breath when he breathes out, breathes her own air into him as he breathes in. This is how they keep each other alive.

In the deepest part of every night, Ernie gasps suddenly, throws his arms up and thrashes wildly. Sometimes he whimpers; sometimes he yells, "I won't. Don't!" Then he sits up, his eyes wide open. "Here," he says on a sigh, then lies down again and goes right back to sleep.

After Ernie calms down, Amanda stares at the dark spot in front of her where she imagines his eyes are. "There's nothing to be afraid of," she whispers. "Nothing at all." She breathes in time with him once more to still their wild hearts – because, now that Judy has gone, Amanda has discovered she is afraid after all.

Amanda worries about the parts of the house she's not in and can't see. When it begins to get dark, she sits in the lounge with all the lights on and her back against the wall so she can see the TV and both doors at once. There are dark places in the house now – places she won't go, where the outside has seeped in through the gaps in the window frames. She is most afraid of the long hallway, where the front door, made from three panes of frosted glass stacked one on top of the other, is a fragile skin between her and whatever is outside and lurking between the house and the hedge, desperate to get in.

Amanda wakes to a thump-crash and jagged sounds in the hallway. A man's voice – swearing maybe, but indistinct. She scoots off the bed and wedges herself in the closet behind the boxes, breathes through her open mouth and covers her hands with her eyes as if her lack of sight will make her magically disappear.

Then Ernie is in the middle of the room, his tie wrapped around his hand like a bandage, blood all over the sleeve of his jacket and the front of his shirt. Amanda creeps from her hiding place.

"I forgot my keys again and had to break the window." Blood drips from his hand and darkens a spot on the carpet. Amanda nods but doesn't understand. "You shouldn't be up," he says. "It's late. Go to bed. Go to your own bed. You shouldn't be sleeping in here."

Amanda tiptoes out of his room and toward her own bedroom door, then stops and squirms. The hallway is still dark with its burned-out bulb, and worse, there's a blacker spot where the window at the top of the front door used to be. Now all the glass is gone.

The night darkness slithers through the hole. It thickens the air. Amanda can barely breathe. "I can't."

Ernie sighs. "Okay. You can stay here. But go to sleep."

She stays awake until Ernie comes to bed, and after that night, she won't fall asleep before Ernie is home. Until she hears his car in the driveway, she keeps the light on. She keeps her eyes open.

There is knocking and the top of Mrs. Price's head is visible through the hole where the glass should be.

"Amanda, I can see your shadow. Open the door."

Amanda opens the door, but not enough to let Mrs. Price inside. "Dad's at work."

"Work? Last night he came home at quarter to two, and the lights were still on, and you should have been asleep! I try to catch him, but he's never here. Tell him that I want to talk to him." Mrs. Price pushes the door properly open, then takes a step back and peers at Amanda, scans her from head to toe. "You look exhausted and filthy. If he doesn't sort this out, I'm calling the authorities."

· · ·

Amanda knows that sometimes they take children away and put them with other families, and that would be worse than a house full of holes, so after school she cleans the kitchen as best she can and makes scrambled eggs for dinner because she knows how to do it and there happen to be eggs. She showers too, even her neck. Even behind her ears.

She waits for Ernie to come home, watching TV until her eyes are sleepy, then she puts on her nightie because you are supposed to sleep in bed clothes, not day clothes. Her nightie is a very fine light-blue cotton with no sleeves and nearly see-through; it used to be her mother's and is too big and falls to her ankles. Then she waits some more and tries not to think about the front door and the outside coming in. But the more she waits and tries not to think about it, the more she thinks about it, until the outside pours in through the broken window, thick and slow like burnt liquid sugar. She can smell it, she thinks. Sharp and acrid.

In the flimsy nightie, Amanda is nothing but a wisp alone in the dark hallway, a tiny thing, barely there. And it seems reasonable then, or even a good idea, to find her father and make him come home so she doesn't get taken away. So she doesn't disappear altogether, like her mother.

Once she is outside, Amanda is unsure where to go first, so she stands for a few minutes behind the monkey-apple hedge, shivering in the dewy night air, and tries to decide. When she hears the hum of a car coming, she steps onto the pavement in front of the house. Now she won't have to go looking for Ernie after all. When he sees her there, alone in the dark, he'll get out of his car and tell her to go inside, and after that he'll fix the window in the front door so the outside can't come in, and after that he'll be there every night for dinner and tuck her into bed. The car rounds the corner and Amanda lifts her arm to wave – but it's not his car. It doesn't even slow down before disappearing over the hill.

Amanda looks up and down the street. With all the streetlights and the moon sometimes appearing in the cloudy sky, there is light enough to see the outlines of the houses, and the cars, hunched in the driveways like big dogs. Everyone is sleeping, and everything silent. Amanda stares at the Prices' big front window. She thinks she sees the curtain move and waits. But nothing.

Amanda begins to walk, following her bare feet the way they are used to going – along the street to the top of the hill, down the long, gravel driveway to the park. But, as soon as she gets to the bottom of the driveway, she knows it's a bad idea. The park is unlit and full of lumpy shadows. She waits on the edge of the grass. Clive groans a little at her smell, shakes his chain – *shush* – but doesn't bark.

The slow whistle of the rusty hinge reaches Amanda before her eyes adjust, but then she can see the outline of a person on one of the swings. The outline sways slowly above the ground, as if weightless, tilting away from her, then toward her.

"You *are* here?" Amanda rushes forward.

A cigarette tip flares. She stops. Ernie doesn't smoke. He hates it because it smells bad and gives you heart attacks. "A terrible thing," Mrs. Price had said when she'd heard the news. "A terrible thing."

The wind lifts. Amanda's nightgown rises and swirls around her. "Mummy?" The word, thin and breathy, flies into the air.

"I remember you," says a deep voice, rough on the edges. "Want a smoke?" The ember flares again, then makes an arc. "Come closer."

Amanda pushes down her billowing nightie. "I'm trying to find my dad."

"Your dad's not here, is he?" The outline laughs. Takes another drag.

"I thought –"

"Come here. I'll give you a puff."

"I have to go home." She should run, but she feels suspended, as if treading air like water, her feet inches above the ground.

"Not yet." The outline gets off the swing and walks toward her. She can smell his cigarette now, dirty and familiar. "Remember me?"

"My dad," she whispers. Her nightgown twirls in the wind like a ghost.

"There's nobody here but me."

The cigarette burns inches from her face. Amanda inhales and is overtaken by dizziness. Then she can't tell anymore where her body ends and the darkness begins. "Am I still here?"

The outline reaches out to circle what's left of her wrist. But when his hand touches her, she feels it – her own body, solid and real – and she yanks her hand back and sprints up the driveway. Her feet thump hard on the earth as she runs. Behind her, the boy's laughing becomes fainter until it disappears altogether.

On the street, beneath the streetlight, she looks at her body, all in one piece.

"Amanda!" Ernie is running toward her. He swoops her off the ground and holds her tight. She can feel his heartbeat in her own chest. "You were gone when I got home. I've been looking everywhere for you."

"No. I've been looking for you!" Amanda puts her hands on his cheeks, his gravel skin beneath her palms. "I don't know where you are."

"I'm right here," he says. "You disappeared. What –"

"No, *you* disappeared." She smooths the lines around his eyes with her fingers, brushes the tips of his pretty eyelashes. "You. Don't."

She moves her face close to his, breathes in his warm breath, holds it in her body until she thinks her heart will explode.

EVERYTHING HAPPENS FOR A REASON

Clare's father wore short, white sports shorts and a tight, white T-shirt, hair slicked down and shiny, black and hard as a beetle shell. He stood at the front door and tapped the face of his brand new Casio digital wristwatch. "Let's go."

Clare crossed her arms over her chest, then dropped them again immediately because she was tender where she was "developing." Her mother's word. "I hate tennis. I'm not going."

"Don't say 'hate.' It's a bad word." Her father had a dark tan, a thick moustache and hair on the back of his hands, all the way down to his middle knuckles. Clare's mother used to say he was a manly man, handsome, and swore she wasn't proud and just stating a fact, but now she wouldn't talk about him at all. "There are other kids to play with. You'll have fun."

"It's boring, and I hate the kids there too. They're stupid."

Clare's mother had not dressed for church because she said she could not go and show her face. She wore a housedress instead of her Sunday best and twisted a cotton handkerchief between her fingers. Her hands were red and peeling from doing the washing up. She had the water scalding hot, and since Kevin left, she wouldn't use gloves, ever, said she couldn't even feel it, but Clare heard her wince every time she put her hands in the steaming sink. "You have to go. He's your father."

"I promise she'll be back by five," Kevin said. "We have a late game."

"We?" Clare said.

"Don't be later than that, Kevin. Don't." Clare's mother worried all the time now about everything and wouldn't leave the house anymore unless she had to.

Kevin nodded, staring dully over Clare's mother's shoulder to the end of the hall, where Clare had left the bathroom door wide open on purpose, so anyone could see the toilet with its fluffy, lavender seat-cover and the swan-shaped toilet-bowl cleaner brush beside it. Her mother didn't notice things like that now and hadn't even told Clare off or pulled the door shut when she had walked by it to answer the door.

Clare followed her father down the front stairs to the driveway. From the bottom step, she could see that Kevin's new girlfriend, Gabby Dee, was in the passenger seat of his new car, her sneakered feet up on the dashboard. She swished her bleach-blond ponytail to whatever was on the radio.

"Not with her."

"Manners," Kevin said. He sighed. "Try. Okay?"

Clare glared back at his lopsided smile.

When Clare got into the back seat, Gabby turned and wiggled her fingers. "Nice to meet you. Kevin has told me so much about you." Her voice was low and smooth, not the girlish voice Clare had been expecting. Clare put her hands over her ears. Gabby's mascara was clumped on her bottom lashes, and her frosted-pink lipstick was smeared slightly above her top lip. "You like horses, don't you? And reading. That's what your dad said."

Gabby Dee was twenty-three, nineteen years younger than Clare's father and twelve years older than Clare. She used to be a singer in their church worship band, but after she and Kevin ran off together, they stopped going to church. Now Gabby sang Fleetwood Mac covers on Saturday night at the Milford Hotel lounge bar, and Clare's father sat at a table near the front and nodded along, according to Fiona's sister, who saw them there every weekend when she went drinking, even though she was too young to drink. "He looks like her proud dad," Mimi had told her. "It's sweet."

As the car reversed down the driveway, Clare's mother remained standing at the open front door, blank-faced, while she snaked the handkerchief, up and down, between her fingers and around her wrists, as though she were trying to tie her own limbs in knots.

"You've just started at intermediate school, haven't you?" Gabby turned again and bounced up and down a little in her seat. "I wish I was still in school. We would have been friends, don't you think?"

"Look." Clare pointed to a concrete veranda where a shirtless, fat old man, pale and bulbous as a lump of lard, fanned himself with a folded newspaper. "Is he your type?"

"You never know!" Gabby giggled. "Right, Daddio?" She tickled Kevin's ribs. Instead of swatting her hand away, he grabbed her fingers and held her palm against his ribs.

Clare watched the fat man for a long time out the back window, until he was maggot-sized, then pretended to squash him between her forefinger and thumb.

"You'll have to entertain yourself, at least for a while." Kevin's eyeball floated in the rear-view mirror. "We have a tournament today. Don't get into any trouble."

"I never get into trouble." The tips of Clare's fingers throbbed. She had bitten her nails so far down they were unchewable, and she'd had to move on to her nail-bed skin. Her ring finger had begun to bleed. "Ever." She licked off the blood, then sucked her finger to soothe the pain.

"Why don't you watch us play?" Gabby said. She half-whispered to Kevin, "I can't wait for the mixed doubles," as though she meant something else, not tennis, and Clare was not supposed to notice. Kevin slid a hand over and trickled his fingers along Gabby's smooth, bare thigh.

"My mother wears pantyhose every day, even in the summer." Clare leaned between the two front seats. Kevin withdrew his hand. "She says bare legs are cheap."

"Is that so! Aren't you just boiling though, in that outfit?"

It was the very end of summer, cold now in the evenings, but sunny and humid at the height of the day. Although Clare's mother had pointed to the wall thermometer and wanly suggested a T-shirt and skirt – bare legs below the knee being acceptable for children – Clare wore corduroys held up with a shiny, plastic belt; a long-sleeved, button-down shirt; and sandals. Everything pink. She didn't like other people to see her pale and freckled skin, her goosebumps or the thin blue veins branching at her wrists. She especially didn't want them to see how the hair on her arms and legs was beginning to thicken and darken. She didn't like to see it herself. She had experimentally shaved her legs a few weeks earlier, without her mother knowing, and the hair had grown back wiry and blunt-ended and much more noticeable.

"So blond. Pretty," Gabby said. "You should try to get a bit of sun though. Come out onto the court for a bit. I can lend you a T-shirt if you want; it doesn't matter if it's too big." She winked at Clare in the mirror. "You'll get there one day!" Clare's throat tightened in that way it did right before she had to vomit.

As they drove down the gravel driveway to the tennis club, through the bush reserve that surrounded the courts, Clare said over and over, "You'll both lose anyway," but silently, so Kevin and Gabby couldn't hear her.

Station wagons crammed the clubhouse car park. "We're late," Kevin muttered. It always annoyed him to have to park far from his destination, as though it were a comment on his importance. Redness creeped up the back of his neck as he pivoted the steering wheel and squeezed the car into a tight space in a clearing at the edge of the bush.

"Aw, Daddio," Gabby simpered and stroked his arm. "Don't be grumpy."

Clare's father smiled at Gabby in a way Clare had never seen him smile at her mother – with his eyes too soft and liquid.

Clare thrust open the car door, but instead of getting out, she kicked her feet hard against the back of Gabby Dee's seat and hummed tunelessly for a few seconds. "I think I'll just stay here, Kevin," Clare said at last. "In the car." She would stay there all day, perish from dehydration in the heat. That would teach them.

"Don't call me Kevin!" he snapped, then took a deep breath. "C'mon, Clare, please? What about if we get you an ice cream afterward?"

Gabby nodded along as if she had some say.

"Three scoops." Clare jumped out and flung the car door closed behind her. "Okay, Kevin?"

"Clare, how many times have I told you not to slam?"

"How many times have I told you blah blah blah?" Clare mimicked, but he didn't hear her. He was already ahead, hand in hand with Gabby, and Clare had to trail behind them, alone.

The clubhouse was the top floor of a two-storey shoebox topped with a sloped, corrugated iron roof and a long window across the front that gave a clear view of the six asphalt courts below. There was a kitchen at the far end with a huge boiler and upside-down cups and plates of Vanilla Wine biscuits set out on the counter. The tournament hadn't started, and the room was crowded with players. The men stood in small groups, lightly swinging their racquets and laughing too loudly with their heads thrown back and mouths wide open. Amanda's dad was there too, laughing last, as if he didn't get the joke and was pretending. The ladies twirled around the room handing out cups of tea or collecting the empties. They were nearly identical in their bobble socks and white minidresses and tennis knickers in pastel shades, frilly on the bum. They all had bare legs.

Kevin and Gabby made their way through the room. A few men said hello to Kevin and Amanda's dad smiled stupidly at Gabby, but all the wives ignored the couple entirely. No one offered them tea.

Clare searched the room for Amanda – she would do, if there was no one better – but she wasn't there. She leaned back against the kitchen counter and watched the other children, but they were all much younger than she was. They wheeled aimlessly between the adults' legs, crawling their sticky fingers over thighs and furniture. Every now and then, one of the children was patted, or lifted and snuggled and kissed. Clare could not recall either of her parents kissing her, not even goodnight. Once, when Clare was much younger, she had experimentally put her arms around her mother's waist when her mother stood at the bathroom mirror powdering her face. Her mother had waited a few seconds before stepping away. Then she had tapped Clare lightly on top of the head with her fingertips. "We're not that kind of family," she had said to Clare's reflection. "My mother didn't hug me either."

Kevin and Gabby were at the blackboard to find out what court they would be playing on. Gabby stretched her arm around Kevin and leaned against him heavily. She was petite and much smaller than him. Someone might think she was his daughter, in here, where parents and children were openly affectionate – except that everyone knew that Gabby was Kevin's girlfriend. Clare's mother had told Clare the whole neighbourhood knew about it and all the parents at Clare's school. And everybody at church, of course.

Clare tugged at her shirt, wrapped her arms around her upper body and wished she were anywhere else.

A bell sounded. The players began to jostle one another out the door.

"Don't go anywhere," Kevin commanded on his way out. "I don't want to have to be looking for you when it's time to leave. I'll never hear the end of it from your mother if I get you home late."

"Where would I go?"

"See ya!" Gabby chirped. "Have fun! Come and watch if you feel like it." She bounced out ahead, and Kevin tapped her behind with his racquet.

A few minutes later, Clare was alone in the clubhouse with two boys who sprawled on the sofa reading comics and a small group of girls who sat in a circle on the floor and manoeuvred their half-dressed Barbies with tiny hops from imaginary house to imaginary house.

Clare went to the window. A few of the games had started, but Kevin and Gabby were still making their way to the farthest court with another couple. Kevin waved his racquet around his head, and the other man laughed and slapped Kevin on the back. Gabby tossed her ponytail and half-walked, half-skipped beside him. The other woman walked ahead, alone.

At the other end of the courts, farthest from where Kevin and Gabby were now positioning themselves, the car park was edged by a stretch of dense, green-black bush that dipped into the ravine, then rose and covered the side of the hill facing the tennis club. On the farthest side of the bush, cookie-cutter houses on the edge of the new subdivision sat on top of the ridge.

Kevin and Gabby were playing now; Kevin at the back of the court, Gabby at the net. Clare was surprised they played so well together. Gabby was quick and her father was powerful. If they won, they would move on and play for the entire afternoon, non-stop, until the final at the end of the day.

"Oooh, I love you, baby," one of the little girls trilled as she and another girl waved their Barbies at each other. "Let's kiss. Let's make babies, baby." They smashed their two Barbies' bodies together and made smooching noises.

Kevin served and the ball hit the net. He threw the second ball up in the air and swung his racquet. The ball sliced into the far opposite corner of the court. His opponent missed it.

Clare surveyed the bush. How far could she get before Kevin figured out she was missing? Would he come looking for her? If she stayed out long enough, they would have to call the police. Clare's mother would be so upset, Clare would never have to spend time with Kevin and Gabby again.

The little girls chatted and hummed and fiddled with their Barbies' tiny clothes. The boys stared, unblinking, at the bright pages of their comics.

Clare opened the clubhouse door and stood on the threshold. "I'm going for a walk," she said to no one in particular, and no one paid the slightest attention.

At the trailhead, a nearly hidden sign explained the extent of the reserve. It covered a large basin and was bisected by a creek, the central artery of trickling streams along its length. The bush had been maintained after the surrounding land was cleared for the courts and the subdivision, the sign said. It was inhabited by native birds and trees, and, if you looked closely, wetas, grubs and spiders. From where Clare stood, where the bush and the car park met, the houses on the upper ridge were still clearly visible, but anyone could see that the reserve was big enough to get lost in. The paths were marked, the sign said, but there was no map.

As Clare read the information board, voices rose from somewhere close within. Laughter, then a deep voice. "I'll get you!" the voice roared. "Grrrr. I'll get you."

A child shrieked happily.

Clare started on the uneven, dirt track and began the descent toward the creek. In less than a minute she was bathed in a fine coolness and the world outside the bush disappeared.

Spindly manuka trees with ragged light-grey bark lined the path. The bark reminded Clare of peeling sunburned skin. She ran her hand along one of the trunks and shuddered. There were black-trunked punga too, low ferns and tall nikau palms, their dry fronds rattling like bones in the light breeze that spun above the canopy. Invisible birds called to one another, first pretty and bell-like, then with territorial creaking and cawing. In a small clearing, the sun glared, and in an instant, the coolness was gone. Clare's clothes were already damp with humidity and sweat and stuck to her skin. She pulled at her training bra and noted the dull ache in her breasts that she had been trying to ignore all morning.

Every now and then, Clare could hear the voices of the picnickers above the close and quiet sounds that surrounded her, but after she had been walking for a while, the voices disappeared, and the creek's burble increased. The creek must have been running high from the recent three days of solid rain – the path was still sticky with mud and the ground at the edges of the path was sodden and swampy and large, blue-black flies buzzed heavily over shallow pools of stagnant water. Clare imagined the flies' feet trickling over her skin.

At the first fork in the track, there was nothing to tell Clare which way to go besides a pair of red and blue triangles pointing in opposite directions, so she continued downward and tried to remember the path she had taken as she went. By the fifth fork, she couldn't recall the sequence of turns, or the way back. She kept onward, anyway, following the track toward the sound of the water.

When she reached the edge of the creek she stopped. "Hello?" she yelled, to try it out. She waited. "Hello?"

After walking for ten more minutes or so, she moved away from the path and onto the spongy creek bank, tracing the creek's curves always farther downward, until finally it disappeared into a wide, plastic pipe buried in the earth and there was nothing left to follow. Clare scrambled up the bank, looking for the path, but after climbing though a tangle of trees she was met by a sudden clearing, strewn with dusty gravel and bleached by the hard glare of the afternoon sun. At the centre of the clearing, all wrong in the bright sunlight, stood a small hut.

Clare crept in a circle around the building's edge and breathed in the fresh-wood smell of its plywood walls. The hut looked like it had been hastily constructed and was not quite square. A corrugated iron roof dangled over the front wall. It didn't have any windows, just a door with a sliding lock and a heavy padlock, the kind you need a little key for.

Clare rapped on the door and a tui cackled loudly in response from the treetops. She jumped back.

Her heart thumping, she waited for a few moments, then pulled a slide out of her hair and poked it in the lock. She imagined it would be easy – when they did it on TV, it wasn't so hard – but she couldn't even get the hairclip into the opening, let alone use it to pop the mechanism. She kicked the bottom of the door hard a few times, then yanked down on the padlock. It clicked open.

Sunlight through the open door revealed a dirt floor, an aluminum beach chair and, along the back wall, a counter, also plywood. On the counter, some tools: A hammer, a jar of nails, a saw. Wire on a reel. Screws and a screwdriver. A used tin of paint, a bottle of turpentine and some rags. One dirty mug.

Clare entered, pulled the door shut behind her and sat down on the chair.

The walls muffled the sounds of the bush, and the only light filtered finely through the gaps between the plywood sheets and illuminated floating dust, pollen and strands of cobweb in thin streaks.

Clare put her hands in her lap and crossed her feet at the ankles. She could wait in the hut until twilight, then find her way back, maybe make her way through the bush to a house on the ridge as though she had got lost, then call her mother directly.

Ever since Kevin had left, Clare's mother never got mad. All day, she wandered around the house, cleaning listlessly, the venetians down and tilted strategically so the neighbours couldn't spy. But her mother would be frantic by the time Clare called her. Angry for once. Livid. She would blame Kevin.

Clare closed her eyes.

Amplified by the iron roof, the measured tapping of the first drops of rain woke Clare from a dreamless sleep. Almost immediately the rain started to crackle and pop, then crash on the roof. Within less than a minute, rivulets of water crept under the bottom of the walls and snaked around the chair. Clare lifted her feet.

After the rain had been drumming persistently for five or six minutes, the door swung open, and Gabby, soaked from head to toe, threw herself inside. "You're here! I've been looking for you." She shook herself, then twisted and squeezed her sopping ponytail. "How come you're dry?" Her wet tennis whites were nearly see-through. She wore a lacy bra.

"Go away!"

"I went up to the clubhouse to find you between games and you weren't there."

"So?"

"I was worried." Gabby pulled her wet clothes away from her body while she turned fully around and examined the hut. She was slim, but curvy. Clare tried not to look. "Someone has been here."

Gabby picked up the mug, then put a finger against her cheek. She narrowed her eyes theatrically, teasing. "Or did you come to meet someone?"

"Don't be stupid."

"I've known girls like you." Gabby wandered to the back of the hut. "You act like you don't care about what anyone thinks of you." She stopped behind Clare and lifted her hair, smoothed it with her nails at the scalp, then gathered it into a ponytail in her fist. "Act like you want to be invisible." She curled around to see Clare from the front. "But you don't. No one does."

Clare yanked her hair out of Gabby's hand and jumped off her chair, which fell over behind her with an empty clang. "My mother says you're a slut."

Gabby leaned back against the counter. She lifted and set down the tools one by one. "You're no better than me."

"Well, are you?"

"You're so lucky and you don't even know it." Gabby picked up the hammer and weighed it, then smacked it heavily back on the counter. "I never even had a dad." A hard edge had come into her voice.

"Now I don't either!" Clare stamped her foot and began to cry.

"You do so." Gabby jumped toward her and for a moment, Clare was afraid, but Gabby leaned forward and wrapped her arms softly around Clare's shoulders. "What about if we could be like sisters? I always wanted a sister, didn't you?"

"Ugh. Get off me." Clare pushed Gabby away roughly, and Gabby tumbled backward onto the dirt floor in her sodden bright whites and was instantly covered in mud. Clare leaped to the doorway. "You're a bad person. You should be punished." She went out into the rain and slammed the door behind her. Clicked the padlock shut.

"Clare!" Gabby rattled the door and laughed. "Come on! Don't leave me in here."

Gabby thought it was a joke. She thought everything was joke.

"There are consequences, you know!" Clare thumped the lock against the door. "I can't open it now, even if I wanted to. Now you can find out what it's like to be all alone."

"I already know what that's like," Gabby said.

Clare set off into the bush. The rain poured down through the trees and bounced off the leaves. The track was nearly obliterated by swirling, muddy puddles. A massive clap of thunder seemed to shake the branches all around her, and a few seconds later the darkening bush flashed with lighting. It wasn't a warm summer storm either. A freezing wind had picked up and the raindrops were sharp and cold.

Clare pushed her soaking hair back off her face, but it did no good. The solid rain and dim light made it difficult to see. In her flimsy sandals, she splashed through the puddles and stumbled on hidden roots. When she reached out toward narrow tree trunks to steady herself, they bent under her weight and tipped her sideways. She slipped and floundered on the muddy ground. Every now and then she stopped and tried to get her bearings, but once she was above the line of the creek, she realized she could be anywhere. She had followed the water down – but was it this feeder stream, or another one? It was impossible to tell which side of the basin she was on. Freezing cold and covered in mud, she tried to find her way back to the creek, but ended up at a fork, where water rushed down from two different directions.

The rain fell harder still, and sheet lightning flashed right above the bush, illuminating for a few seconds the dark path.

She continued to stumble through the bush for what seemed like a long time until she was again at the fork where the two streams met. But was it the same fork? It might have been on higher ground, but she wasn't sure.

On the next step, her foot slipped from under her, and her

ankle twisted sideways. She yelped with pain but couldn't even hear her own voice over the racket of the storm. She pulled herself off the path and sat down against a punga, hoping its arching fronds would give her some protection, then cried and shivered until her teeth rattled.

Out of well-trained habit, she clasped her hands against her chest. "Please, God," she said. "Help me get out of here. If you do, I'll tell them where Gabby is. I'll tell my dad the truth. I swear."

She peered down the dark path; nothing but rain. "Help!" she bleated through a pinched throat, even though she knew no one would hear it, not even God.

God had never listened to her anyway. If He had, her father wouldn't have left. She had prayed nightly, bargaining with the little she had. She had vowed silence in school, obedience at home. For an entire week, she had walked with a stone carefully placed in her shoe and still had a deep purple bruise on the sole of her foot to prove it. But Kevin had gone, and everyone knew why, and now her mother was somehow absent, even when she was there. How could God have allowed it?

"Why don't you care about me?" She kicked her twisted ankle against a tree on purpose and swore.

"Clare!" Kevin, aglow in his whites, materialized on the path ahead, then ran toward her. "I told you not to go anywhere!" Rain streamed down his face, and his hair was no longer smooth and shiny, but curly like it used to be.

"I want to go home!"

Kevin shook her a little. "Where is she?"

"Who?"

"Gabby!"

"Were you looking for me?"

"Was she with you?"

"I hurt my ankle."

"She's bare-legged. No sleeves. She could get hypothermia in this weather." Kevin grabbed Clare's hand and pulled her through the near-dark bush behind him. "Did you see her?"

"My ankle," Clare said. But Kevin couldn't hear her over the rain.

Clare had fallen close to the trailhead, and they made it to the car park in a couple of minutes. Once they were clear of the bush, Kevin let go of Clare's hand and hurried ahead, expecting her to keep up. She hobbled behind him, and by the time she had arrived at the clubhouse, Kevin was already on the phone, talking to the police.

"Dad?" She pulled on his arm. "Dad?"

He hung up the phone. "This is your fault. I told you to stay put." Kevin returned to the storm.

"My fault?" She wouldn't tell him. He deserved it.

One of the mothers bundled Clare up in a blanket and drove her home. As she slid around the back seat on the winding driveway that led up to the main road her stomach lurched.

Clare's mother was waiting for her by the front door, as if she had not moved a step from when Clare left in the morning, except now her blank stare had been replaced by drawn eyebrows that could have meant anger or worry, or both. "It's well past five," she called out, when she saw Clare coming up the path with the woman, both huddled under a single umbrella. "Is everything all right?"

"She wandered off and got soaked," the woman said. "Kevin's lost his little girlfriend. He's still there, looking for her. Silly cow. What a commotion."

"I hurt my ankle," Clare said.

"Go and get changed." Clare's mother pushed Clare into the hallway.

"I think I need a bandage."

"You need to wash yourself. You're dirty all over." Clare's mother tut-tutted while Clare limped to the bathroom.

"You see?" Clare's mother said later, when she came to say good night. "Things work out the way they are supposed to. People get what they deserve in the end because God is keeping account."

Clare's mother flicked off the light, then leaned down, smoothed the hair back off Clare's face and, for the first time that Clare could remember, softly kissed her on the cheek.

The following Sunday, Clare was startled to see Kevin at the front door in his tennis whites.

"But, Gabby –" She had been sure he would not want to see her again, after what she had done.

"Don't worry me like that again, okay?"

"You were worried about me?"

Kevin tapped his watch. "What do you think? Come on."

Clare's mother appeared. "Off you go." She was dressed in her best navy suit and pumps. "You can't stay here by yourself. I'm going to church."

Gabby was in the front seat of the car with the stereo turned up loud.

"We're going to teach you how to play today," Kevin said, once Clare was in the back seat. "Gabby's idea. Keep you both busy so you don't get lost again." He chuckled as though it had all been a game.

Gabby's blond ponytail bobbed up and down in front of Clare's nose. "I wasn't lost!" she laughed. She turned and waved newly pink painted nails at Clare. "Your hair looks so pretty."

Clare patted her own ponytail. "Oh. Thanks." She wriggled in her seat. Smoothed the top of her skirt. "They found you?"

"Well, duh! I was nice and dry in that hut." Gabby winked at Clare.

"I was worried," Clare said. "I didn't mean – I didn't –" Her eyes began to well. God knew the truth. It didn't matter what she said now.

"I've always had to look after myself. You don't ever need to worry about me. Kevin was just making a big fuss about nothing. I was totally fine."

"Best place for you, I guess. It could have been bad for you, Gabrielle, if you had ended up wandering around in the bush in that storm," Kevin said.

"Like me," Clare whispered, ashamed. Her chest burned. Her mother was right – God was keeping account, but not how she thought.

The fat man was on his porch as they drove by, shirtless again, his body soft and pale as a newborn baby. Was he really alone, or was there someone inside who loved him? He stretched his arms above his head to sun himself and smiled.

Gabby rolled down the window, leaned out a little and freed her ponytail. Illuminated by the bright sun, her hair blew around her head like flames licking the pure air.

"Everything happens for a reason." Gabby turned and smiled at Clare. Her face glowed. She was beautiful.

Clare fell back against her seat as if she had been pushed, slapped her forehead and laughed so hard she nearly peed herself.

AMANDA'S BAPTISM

Amanda lay face down on her unmade bed in the path of a small desk fan turned on high and read a Harlequin romance she had bought at the second-hand shop for ten cents. She had already devoured the book twice, so although she had only been reading for a couple of hours, she had already got to the part where Ashley gives herself up to the irresistible pull of the mysterious Dante when there were three short raps on the metal frame of the screen door. Amanda would have ignored the knocking and pretended she wasn't there, but the front door was open because of the heat, so it was obvious someone was home. She would have to answer it. Another knock came, louder this time, then the clicking of impatient feet in hard-soled shoes.

Amanda pushed herself off the bed, leaned out of her bedroom and squinted down the hallway. Behind the screen stood a pair of crewcut men in short-sleeved white shirts, long grey pants, polished shoes and navy-blue-and-black-striped neckties. It wasn't their outfits, name badges or even the books they held, but their orthodontically enhanced teeth that gave the men away immediately as Mormon missionaries. Only Americans had such perfect teeth, and the only Americans that ever came to the front door in New Zealand were Mormons. Everyone knew that.

When she stepped into the hallway proper, Amanda faced the Mormons but was far enough away from the door to seem to have not quite answered it yet. She wore a green halter top that tied around her neck and back with thin strings and her shortest denim short shorts; it was the school holidays, and too hot for anything else, but when she stood in front of the two young men, immaculate in their white shirts, she was squeamish suddenly, uncomfortable, as though she had forgotten to put on her underwear. She tugged at the bottom of her cut-offs.

The taller missionary was pale with glossy, blond, nearly shaved hair, behind which his deeply sunburned scalp glowed pink. He cleared his throat. "How are you today?" His smile was unfaltering and rigid, and made him seem not quite real, but his voice was tender, with round *R*s, like a movie star. "Hi there!" he tried again. "We wondered if we could come in and sit a few minutes and talk with your family about Joseph Smith and the *Book of Mormon*."

If she didn't respond, perhaps they would just leave. Clare's dad used to say that the wrong words could let the devil in, and he had chastised Amanda once when she'd said "just my luck" because if you believed in luck, you ignored God's power. When Mormons had come knocking at his house, he had instructed his family to hide by crouching together beneath the big picture window. Then they waited for the Mormons to be on their way because they were not going to invite the devil through their front door. Mr. Price was a real Christian, not the Mormon kind. At least, until he ran off with a woman from church and stopped being any kind of Christian at all.

The second Mormon leaned forward and said, "Is your mother home?" He was good-looking in a baby-faced kind of way and not as severe as the other in appearance, with dark, wavy hair and gentle auburn eyes.

"It's just my dad. My mother's dead," Amanda said. She had learned it was better to explain right away to avoid any confusion in the future, although the immediate admission had its own complications. Usually, the other person would say then, "I'm sorry," and Amanda would tell them it wasn't their fault, which wasn't quite right, but she couldn't piece together what "I'm sorry" meant exactly. Worse, this exchange always left the terrible question up in the air: Then whose fault was it?

But the Mormon didn't apologize. He rocked back on his heels and glanced sideways at his friend before he gazed at Amanda directly. "That's awfully sad. You must feel lonesome without your mother." "Lonesome" – an American word.

The blond slipped his books under his arm, steepled his fingers in front of his chest, then bowed his head and peered up at Amanda from beneath his translucent eyebrows. "It's only our Lord Jesus who really helps us through at times like that." Then he whispered something.

Amanda came closer. "I'm sorry?"

"I said, do you trust in God?"

Amanda gripped the handle of the front door. "My dad's not here right now. You'll have to go."

While the Mormons descended the stairs, Amanda twisted her halter top sideways to unstick it from her damp skin, and the ties loosened and came undone. Babyface turned just as Amanda's top fell and she caught it and clutched it against her chest. His face bloomed bright pink, but he gave a short wave and said, "Well. It was so nice to meet you. We'll see you later," as if he hadn't noticed.

"Okay." Amanda struggled to retie her top, confused about whether or not she had agreed to their coming back.

Once they were safely gone, Amanda decided to change into her bikini and spend the rest of the afternoon in the back garden on the sun lounger listening to music though the Walkman her dad had just bought her for Christmas because she asked for it, not because he knew what to buy. Her best friend Margie had made her a mixtape to go with it. Margie had just moved to the neighbourhood and had been teaching Amanda about music ever since she found Amanda listening to Madonna. "Oh my God!" she had shrieked. "That is so not cool. Madonna's for kids." Now she was educated about music, Amanda thought there was too much Bon Jovi and not enough Joy Division on Margie's tape, but it was loud. If anyone came, she wouldn't hear them.

By eight o'clock, Amanda had given up on Ernie's coming home for dinner. Still in her bikini, and now horribly sunburned, she buttered some white bread and slapped together a pickled-beetroot sandwich. She was getting ready to eat it in front of the TV when the Mormons returned. They called through the screen door, like they were old friends over for a visit. "Hey there! We were just on our way back from seeing Mr. Clark."

Mr. Clark had invited Amanda over once, to babysit, he had said, but when she arrived, both his wife and baby were out. "Call me John," he'd said. Then he'd suggested they read some magazines together instead – not just *Playboys*, he had told her, but the more "detailed kind." He'd rifled through the pages of a magazine to show her what he meant.

Amanda had fidgeted and only glanced at the photographs, abstractions of naked bodies in positions that made no sense to her. Mr. Clark had told her to sit, then sat down too, picked up another magazine, moved closer, groaned when she shifted awkwardly beside him. He wore walk shorts, and when he pushed his bare leg against Amanda's, she jumped as though she had been given an electric shock. "Thank you for having me," she had squeaked. "But I don't feel well." He didn't bother seeing her to the door.

Mrs. Clark left for good soon after that, and Amanda had felt guilty then because it seemed to her that Mr. Clark had needed something from her, attention or understanding, and if she had given it, Mrs. Clark and the baby might have stayed.

"Yes. We had a wonderful chat with Mr. Clark," the voice said. "Hello?" The TV exploded with applause and synthesizer music.

"Could we trouble you for a glass of water?" Amanda flicked off the TV and went to the door.

The sun was low in the sky and beat down on the Mormons' backs. A fat sweat drop trickled down Babyface's temple, and both men now had dark patches under the arms of their previously crisp white shirts. They couldn't have been more than nineteen or twenty. She would turn fifteen in a couple of weeks. She wished she had put her clothes back on after sunbathing.

"Yes," the taller Mormon said, the blond one. "It sure is hot out here in the sun."

The other wiped his glistening forehead with the back of his hand.

Amanda opened the screen door and led them into the living room. "Wait a minute." She left them there, giant-sized in the cramped room, their hands full of books and satchels, while she went to get glasses of water.

She found her shorts in the kitchen where she had left them and put them on over her bikini bottoms, then turned the tap and waited for the warm water that had been sitting in the pipes to clear. It sounded cheap, somehow, that running tap.

When she returned the Mormons were examining the framed photos on the mantelpiece, mostly of Amanda and Judy when they were kids. Judy had found the photos in a long-forgotten box when Amanda and Ernie moved after Ernie's separation from Helen, his second wife. "Now someone actually lives here," Judy had said when she propped up the photos. "A family." A few days after that, Judy had followed her boyfriend on a year-long trek through Africa.

The blond Mormon drank the water quickly, his Adam's apple sliding up and down with every gulp. When he was finished, he placed the empty glass carefully on a coaster Amanda and Ernie never used, then took one of the photos from the mantel and brought it close to his face. "You have a sister."

"Judy. She's away." The last postcard had been from Rwanda. They were going to see gorillas.

"You were a very pretty child." He turned the photo so his partner could see. Amanda was chubby, highly freckled, with too-large new adult teeth, her hair cut crookedly across her forehead. When the photo was taken, her mother had been dead for two months. Amanda had studied this photo often, trying to decipher what she must have been feeling, or if she had felt anything at all. "How old are you here? Seven? Eight?" He looked directly at her. "You still are, of course. Pretty, I mean."

Babyface coughed and shifted his weight from one foot to the other. His partner picked up another photo and showed it to her. "Your mother?"

Amanda nodded.

"You have the same dark hair and eyes."

"I'm Elder Young." Babyface extended his hand.

Amanda's own hand was sticky. She waved it in the air as if to dry it off, then Elder Young encased her narrow fingers and pumped up and down for a few seconds. "This is Elder Call." Elder Call returned the photo of Amanda's mother then shook her hand too. They stood awkwardly then, waiting.

"And you?" Call asked her at last. "What's your name?" She told them, and then he questioned her, using the name she had just given him. "Oh. Do you know what that means, Amanda? 'Deserving of love.' My sister's name." He tilted his head to the side. "How old were you when your mother passed away, Amanda? I'm guessing you must have been quite young."

"I was seven. But . . ." Elder Call waited, but Amanda wasn't sure what she had intended to say.

"I'm sorry," Elder Call said finally, then lowered his eyes. His partner sighed deeply.

"I should go and get dressed now." Amanda moved toward the

door, but Call stepped sideways and blocked her exit. "Amanda, do you know that Mormons know something very special?"

It was like being at the edge of a cliff. If she didn't step back, any minute she would want to jump. She should ask them to leave. Instead, she shook her head slowly, as though hypnotized.

"We know that we'll reunite with our families in heaven, and that we'll always be a family." He towered over her. "Did you know that your mother resides with God, waiting for you, and that you can be with her for all of eternity?" He let that sink in. "The Lord told Joseph Smith that 'the same sociality which exists among us here will exist among us in eternity, only it will be coupled with eternal glory.' Do you understand what that means?"

"When I die, I'll see my mother again."

"So smart! Yes, Amanda. It means that if you accept Jesus Christ into your heart and follow the example of Joseph Smith, then one day in the afterlife you can be with your mother, forever." There was a sudden crunch of gravel from the driveway, but Elder Young continued in the same even tone. "Even if she was not saved when she was alive, we can save her, *you* can save her, now, from this life." A car door slammed.

"Maybe you could come back some other time, okay?" Amanda's father would come through the back door. She tried to shepherd the Mormons to the front, but Elder Young halted and dug around in his bag for a few seconds. He extracted a thick book.

"Here's a copy of *The Book of Mormon*. You can keep it. We'll be back this way next week. Let's talk about what you read next time we meet."

"What's going on?" Ernie had appeared in the dining room. He frowned at the two Americans. "Mormons?" He plunked his briefcase on the table.

Elder Call extended his hand. "I'm –"

"You're leaving."

"Dad!"

Elder Young moved slowly backward, his eyes on the ground.

"Amanda invited us in." Call held his ground and stared at Amanda's father, his lips stretched back, teeth fully exposed, in a kind of smile. "She needs –"

"She doesn't need you."

As soon as he said it, Amanda knew Ernie was wrong. She did need them; the Mormons had come here for a reason. Everything had a reason, everyone had said so after her mother had died, and Amanda had to believe it. How could she not? "It's not up to you."

"I'm your father," Ernie said, hopelessly.

"We should go." Young was already in the hallway.

"Should we?" Elder Call turned to Amanda.

She looked away.

"Take some time to read our book, Amanda," Elder Call said as she followed them out. "You might find some of the solace you've been seeking."

Amanda only nodded, so her father wouldn't know she had agreed.

Solace. How did he know she needed it, when until that moment she hadn't known it herself?

The same time the following week, the Mormons rapped on the screen again, and Amanda wondered about the coincidence of her father's not being there, the second week in a row. He was often late, but not always, like he used to be. Surely this coincidence – the absence of her father, the arrival of the Mormons – must be God's plan. Didn't he manipulate them all like puppets, arranging everything and putting everyone just where He wanted them? Wasn't it really God who moved her arms and legs to open the door and let the Mormons in? God who moved her mouth to say, "I guess it's okay if you sit down"? God who made her sit still and listen to the Mormons' message?

But Ernie didn't believe in God. "If my dad comes home, can you just go out the front?"

Call curled his lips. "God has come to you, and you must honour Him."

Amanda often thought that God had paid too much attention to her already, but it wasn't as if she had a choice, anyway. When he took her mother, God had destroyed everything around her with a simple flick of his giant wrist. Now his hand was stretched out to her. What else could she do but take it?

When Margie came over a few days later, Amanda insisted she couldn't go anywhere, and Margie couldn't stay. Amanda didn't want to leave in case the Mormons visited, and she didn't want Margie to be there if they did. Amanda couldn't wait to see them again. She felt that she was on the brink of a revelation, but Margie wouldn't understand. Margie was spiritual, not religious. She read tarot cards and waved crystals; she didn't go to church and sing "God songs." That was for losers.

"Come on! Why do you want to stay here? I had to work all day." Margie worked in a store and hated it. She had to wear a uniform and her dad took half her paycheque for booze. But that gave her the other half of the paycheque for cigarettes, so she didn't quit. "You're supposed to be my best friend."

"I can't. My dad said."

"As if. Your dad's never here. Just come for a walk."

Amanda couldn't say no to Margie. Margie was beautiful and sexy and brave and got her way everywhere except at home, where she spent as little time as possible. Amanda was plain and quiet and boring, but Margie needed Amanda to adore her, and Amanda needed Margie because she had no one else.

They sauntered around the block together, arms around each other's waists. Margie smoked and chatted about her job, and Amanda listened. When someone honked or whistled from a passing car, Margie yelled, "Piss off," but both girls liked the attention.

When they got back to Amanda's house, the Mormons were climbing the front stairs. "Oh God. Mormons?" Margie dropped her smoke and ground it out.

Elder Call turned and raised a hand. Amanda's heart raced. She dipped her head. "Let's just keep walking." If Margie knew about the Mormons, she would laugh at her and tell everyone at school about it once the summer was over.

Margie yanked Amanda's T-shirt sleeve. "They were cute though," Margie said when they were well clear. "I love Americans."

The Mormons returned the following day.

"I'm sorry," Amanda said. "About yesterday."

"Friends might not understand at first." Elder Young rested his hand on Amanda's shoulder. She took a step back and he followed, as though they were dancing. "She will when she sees how happy you are." He slid his hand slowly down her upper arm then squeezed gently above her elbow. "You're too young to be so sad."

"I'm not much younger than you."

"Maybe not in years. Just in experience," Young said. "Oh, I mean –" He blushed deeply. "With God." Call's face was stony. "I've wanted to be a missionary my whole life." Young perched on the end of the sofa, opposite to where Call now indicated Amanda sit. "To help people like you."

"Like me?"

Young glanced at Call. "I'm not sure how to put it."

"People who are lost." Call dropped his *Book of Mormon* on the table with force and began the lesson.

. . .

After that, the Mormons visited more regularly. Amanda neglected to tell Ernie about it and lied outright to Margie; she said that Ernie was expecting her to make dinner for when he got home, so she couldn't go out. Margie teased Amanda and asked if she had a secret boyfriend, and Amanda said nothing, to make her think it was true.

Each time the Mormons arrived, they knocked, called out "Yoo-hoo!" then immediately let themselves in, like neighbours. At the beginning of each visit, they accepted tea and told Amanda about their lives at home – their large farms and abundant families. At first, they seemed to be like two people with one voice, but soon it was apparent that Elder Young was less instructive and more earnest. He let Call do most of the talking, but he added his own part with feeling. He stammered sometimes and blushed often. When he took his teacup from Amanda, his hands shook. Call was more confident and serious, and when he held her gaze, Amanda was unable to look away.

There were many things they needed to convey, they told her. It was urgent. Their mission lasted only another few weeks, and before they left, they hoped and prayed that she would take Jesus into her heart "and accept the authority of the *Book of Mormon* and recognize Joseph Smith as the prophet of today's New World," Call said, so solemnly Amanda thought he was joking at first.

What it amounted to was that they wanted her to be baptized. "Without baptism," Elder Young said, "you cannot receive salvation, and you will never be reunited with our Heavenly Father – or your own mother." Amanda loved the way his movie-star accent rolled around in his mouth. As she watched his lips move, a deep pink glow came upon the Elder's face, as if he were on fire within. "To live with God, to meet your mother again, you must be spiritually pure, do you understand?"

Amanda nodded, her own face burning too. Though she didn't understand how or why her spirit had become unclean, she knew it must be true. Ernie's wife Helen had said the same thing to Amanda when she pinned her against the kitchen wall in one of her weekly rages. "You filthy, disgusting, dirty thing," she'd spat. "I bet your mother's glad she's dead."

They warned her that there was very little time to take the gift they were offering. "If you don't do it now, you might lose the chance forever," Call said, "and never see your mother again."

"You want to see her, don't you?" Young cooed.

Amanda's eyes teared at the thought. "Yes." She wanted to believe that Helen was wrong, that her mother wanted to see Amanda as much as Amanda wanted to see her. She had to know.

"Then it's an easy decision."

Each time they visited Amanda after that, they sat a little closer to her, and they asked her again to be baptized: Was she ready? Young held her hand. "You will be so happy that you did it, Amanda. Don't you want to experience bliss?" She nodded and as her hand slipped from his, he brushed her palm with his fine-boned fingers.

One Sunday, a few weeks after the Elders' arrival, Amanda took two buses to the Mormon church on the other side of the city where a man was going to be baptized that morning. She had dressed in the most conservative clothes she could find – a knee-length, pleated skirt that was a size too big (a hand-me-down from Judy), a clean T-shirt, pantyhose and a pair of low-heeled pumps that used to belong to her mother and that Amanda had kept. She skipped her usual black eyeliner and brushed her hair until it was nearly straight.

Ernie was in the back garden when she left. He was shirtless and had a handkerchief knotted at all four corners on top of his head, instead of a hat, to keep off the already blazing sun as he wrestled the mower over the knee-high grass. Though deeply tanned, he was not as toned as he used to be, and his skin slid loosely over his frame as he moved. When he saw Amanda, he stopped mowing and took off the handkerchief and wiped his face with it. His hair was nearly entirely grey. "Where are you going dressed like that?"

"Like what?"

"Did those Mormons come back?"

"I'm going out with Margie." It was easy for Amanda to lie to Ernie because he didn't know who she was. But then, Amanda didn't really know who she was herself. That's why Margie liked Amanda – she was pliable and went along; that was her role. "I don't have any other friends who live close since we moved. Remember?"

"You could have tried to have a better relationship with your stepmother, then we wouldn't have had to move."

"You think it was my fault?"

"Well," Ernie said, as if that explained everything. The lawn mower roared.

The Mormon chapel was a long, low, beige-brick building, punctuated by an angular white spire, front and centre, and surrounded by a shopping-mall-like car park, manicured lawns and neatly shorn shrubs. Elder Young and Elder Call were already at the entrance, and they greeted every person who passed by them with a sober "Welcome, hello." When they saw Amanda, they made a point to say how nicely she was dressed, how grown-up she seemed. Once inside, they shuffled her to the front of the church so that she could observe the events clearly. Amanda sat near the end of the pew, with Young on her left side and Call on her right.

When the service began, congregants rose to speak or lead the hymns. Amanda tried to pay attention, but she was distracted by Elder Young's elbow so close to hers they were nearly touching – though he kept his arm across his body so they would not. She glanced sideways at him and noticed how his pant leg pulled against his thigh muscle, which was tensed like hers, Amanda guessed, so his leg would not graze her own.

After an hour or so, the bishop led a middle-aged man to the baptismal bath – a hard-sided pool, like a kiddy pool, about three feet deep. The man was barefoot and dressed entirely in a white, short-sleeved jumpsuit. He stood knee-deep in the water while the bishop spoke a prayer, then crossed his arms in front of his chest before being dunked backward into the water and then almost immediately pulled up again. As he emerged, water streamed from his clothes and hair. He gasped and trembled and held the bishop to steady himself, but he was resplendent, his face glowing with a golden light.

"Rapture," Elder Call whispered in Amanda's ear. "It makes you feel weightless. Pure spirit."

"I'm a new person!" the man yelled. "Thank you, Jesus."

Amanda had been holding her breath from the time the man had been submerged, but as soon as the man spoke, she gulped a lungful of air and closed her eyes. What would it be like to be born again? Her filthy spirit, clean as a white dove, flying to heaven to meet her mother?

She opened her eyes. Elder Young watched her, the edges of his luminous teeth pressed into his bottom lip. His breathing was louder than usual, and its heat tickled Amanda's neck. There was something about his expression Amanda recognized, but she couldn't quite put her finger on it.

"Bliss," he whispered. "You'll feel it too."

"Yes," said Amanda. She said she would do it next week.

Elder Young beamed. "You're the first soul I've led to God. It will be so special for us both."

Later, Margie called. "Stop ditching me," she whined. "I'm so bored. If you won't meet me at the park, I'll have to ask Fiona to bus over here and she sucks. Are we friends, or what?"

The park was Margie's favourite place – a windswept patch of grass beside a small car park, a set of swings and a metal slide that got too hot for any kid to use after nine in the morning. Tall scrub jagged along the cliff's edge and obscured the view of the dark Pacific and Rangitoto on the horizon. To get to the beach, you had to take three sets of rickety stairs down the cliff face, so almost no one else ever came here. Margie liked it, she said, because it was "bittersweet – and a bit dangerous, like me." She had a flair for the dramatic. When Amanda got there, Margie was on a swing, swishing her bare feet in the sand beneath her and drinking from a large, plastic soft-drink bottle, which she immediately presented to Amanda.

"Look what I've got!" she singsonged. "Vodka. Have some."

"What? No."

"Come on." Margie stilled her swing, pushed the bottle into Amanda's hand and wrapped Amanda's fingers around its neck. "My dad's always too pissed to notice his booze is missing, and yours wouldn't notice if you came home falling over. He wouldn't be there, anyway. Go on. You'll like it."

Before she got to the park, Amanda had wanted to tell Margie that she was going to get baptized, to explain why she had been so busy, but it seemed all wrong now. Margie would make fun of her. Maybe Margie would have partly understood that it was about Amanda's seeing her mother again, if she felt like it, but she couldn't really understand the urgency of fate like Amanda did.

Margie groaned. "I haven't seen you for ages! Don't be boring. You're such a baby."

Amanda took the bottle. Mormons didn't drink alcohol. She'd been taught that early on. But what did it matter if she drank now? She was going to be baptized soon, so she'd never get the chance again. Amanda took a swig from the bottle. "It tastes like Coke."

Margie laughed and grabbed the bottle back. They passed the vodka back and forth, drinking quickly, and by the time they had finished, Amanda was no longer upset and not too scared to swing high, and it was the best feeling in the world to close your eyes and fly through the dewy air like a glistening angel, head back, hair streaming.

After a while, Amanda started to feel sick. She dragged her feet in the sand to stop the swing, then opened her eyes. She was momentarily blinded by harsh daylight, and then for some moments didn't understand the sight that materialized in front of her, across the park: Margie with her back against the slide ladder, two beings, almost identical, in front of her, their faces and hair radiant in the glare of the low sun.

Amanda lurched over to the figures. When she got there, she tried to take hold of the ladder, but stumbled into Margie who laughed and pushed her upright. "Pissed, are ya?" one of the beings said, and then it was clear they were just a couple of teenage boys. One of them passed Margie a joint and she took it and inhaled.

The boys were a little older than Amanda and Margie, sixteen or seventeen. They both had dark mullets, stonewashed jeans, loose white T-shirts and unlaced Nikes, but only one had the faint shadow of a moustache on his upper lip, and the other was more compact, like a muscular dog. Amanda realized it was Kenneth. He used to be a small, lonely boy in her neighbourhood, now he had grown into someone she could barely recognize. Margie hand-ed Amanda the joint. "Go on."

Amanda pretended that she knew what to do. She pinched the joint between her forefinger and thumb and puffed on the end.

Kenneth smiled at Amanda and nodded his head slightly while she held in the smoke and stifled her cough. "Do you like it?"

She nodded, lungs still full of smoke. He snorted with laugh-ter and slapped his thigh. "Hey, Matt, she likes it." The smoke scorched Amanda's chest and throat. She coughed painfully. When he recovered the joint, he grazed his rough fingertips on her palm, and Amanda had the feeling that somehow her hand no longer belonged to her.

"Oh yeah. So, you girls wanna screw?" Matt said, his voice low, like he was joking. Then he leaned close and whispered in Amanda's ear, "Are you a virgin? Huh? Been fucked yet?" He inhaled the joint then blew smoke into Amanda's half-open mouth, like a kiss.

Kenneth sniggered and blushed. "How old are you now, any-way?"

"Old enough, moron." Margie put her arm around Amanda's and tried to turn her away, but Amanda couldn't make her feet move.

"It's better to do it now," Matt said. "Otherwise, how will you know what you've been missing?" He stepped closer to Amanda. She stared at his mouth.

What did God want her to do next?

"C'mon." Margie yanked her out of the boy's grip. "Let's get out of here. Thanks for the weed, losers."

The girls half-jogged, half-staggered hand in hand across the park, the boys hooting and laughing behind them. "You want it! You want it!" one of them yelled. "Bitches!"

When they got to the sidewalk, Margie checked the boys weren't following. They ran for another block until they both collapsed on the verge of the pavement. "Jeez, Mands, I thought you were going to go with him for a minute. He was just messing with you."

"I know!" Amanda said. But she didn't know. She didn't know how you were supposed to say no to the things God put in your way.

"Matt was cute though, eh?" Margie said.

It wasn't up to people to decide. Things happened; unavoidable things. Amanda wobbled to her feet. "I'm going to go to the Celestial Kingdom! I'm going to see my mother."

"What the hell are you talking about?" Margie squinted up at her.

"I'm going to get baptized. By those Mormons."

Margie burst out laughing. Then she stopped and frowned. "Why would you do that? It's bullshit. Your mum's dead, Amanda. It wouldn't change a thing."

"Yes –"

"Oh, except, we couldn't be friends anymore." Margie slapped her arm lightly. "Very funny."

Amanda would have argued with Margie then, for the first time ever, but instead, she vomited on the grass.

Amanda was waiting for the Mormons to arrive on Tuesday afternoon, but Ernie came home first, much too early. He took off his jacket, sighed and pulled at his collar, but said nothing to explain his unusual arrival.

Had God sent him to catch her? Amanda glanced out the window. "Did you forget something?"

"No." He stared at Amanda for too long, rubbed his chin like he'd just been punched. "Those fuckers –" He swivelled his eyes to the window. "Jesus Christ, who's this?"

Amanda caught the flicker of the Elders' white shirts as they passed behind one of the trees in front. It was too late to stop them. She wished they would knock, so she could fake it, but as usual, Elder Young called through the screen for her.

Ernie thrust his chair back from the table. Amanda followed him to the front door.

The Mormons were already in the hallway.

"We're here to see Amanda," Call said. He and Elder Young presented their scintillant teeth to Amanda's father, and suddenly the Americans seemed unfamiliar, strangers, strange. Pristine, identical, but not quite real. Amanda recalled the first time they had visited, wormed their way in. She hadn't let them, had she? A knot tightened in her stomach.

"Maybe you would like to join us?"

Ernie snorted at the offer. "What are you doing in my house?"

"Amanda has been studying with us. She believes she's ready." Elder Young smiled reassuringly at her.

"She's a Presbyterian."

"Amanda has been so sad since the death of your wife," Young said. Ernie put his hands up in front of his face, palms outward, as though he expected the Mormon to hit him. "In heaven, her mother –"

"Her mother was a Presbyterian."

"Amanda has the right to choose salvation for herself." Elder Call pulled himself up. He was taller than her father, and he bent his head down a little before he spoke. "Don't you want her to be happy?"

"I've got enough to worry about without you getting mixed up with all of this, Amanda." Ernie pinched his forehead.

"I can see this isn't a good time." Elder Call began to usher Young out. "Why don't we come back tomorrow?"

"They've downsized me," Ernie said as soon as Amanda shut

the door. "I'll probably have to move. Maybe Wellington. I don't know."

Amanda stamped her foot and began to cry. "I'm going to get baptized next Sunday. I'm going to heaven."

Ernie waved his hands at his side, as though he were in deep water, trying to stay afloat. "Why do you make things so difficult for me?" he said.

Ernie stayed at home all that week, checking the classifieds and calling old contacts. Sometimes he fell asleep on the sofa or sat in a straight-backed chair close to the TV and watched whatever was on. Amanda spent most of her time in the back garden working on her tan. Ernie hadn't finished the lawn, had barely started, and now the grass was getting too long to mow.

The Mormons didn't come. Maybe they came and left again when they saw Ernie's car, or maybe they didn't come at all. Maybe they had discovered the truth about her and understood she wasn't worth it. Maybe she'd just been wrong about the whole thing, and it was better to forget it.

Maybe Helen was right. Amanda was a filthy rag, and her mother was glad she was dead and never wanted to see Amanda again. So maybe it was just as well she wouldn't get to see her in heaven and hear it from her mother's own mouth.

The Saturday before she was supposed to be baptized, the phone rang in the early evening. Amanda's hand and voice shook when she answered, but it was only Margie.

"Are you still talking to me?"

"Of course," Margie said. "Hey, so we're having a little party. Me and some people at this guy's house. Why don't you come over?"

"Are you drunk again?"

"You're not a holy roller yet, are you?" Margie said. "Just come! Jeez! It's probably your last chance ever to have any fun."

Amanda caught the bus to a kitset house in Glenfield on a sloped and treeless lot beside a light industrial park. Heavy metal blared through the open windows. Margie flung open the front door. She wore a loose, ankle-length white dress that was partly see-through and she had a half-drunk bottle of tequila in her hand. Beyond her, Kenneth and his friend from the park were hunched over the glass coffee table, rolling joints, concentrating, heads bobbing in time to the music. They wore the same outfits from the week before.

"I don't know," Amanda said.

"Are you my friend or not?"

Margie pinballed through the kitchen and lounge, then knelt on the floor by the boys. She laughed and winked at Amanda and gestured for her to come. "This is Matt!" She flung a heavy arm across his knee. The boys turned their heads toward Amanda at the same time. "And Kenneth. But you know him, don't you? He said." Kenneth smiled toothlessly, laid his finished joint on the table and rubbed his hands up and down his thighs.

"Sit down, Mands!" Margie held out the bottle of tequila.

Amanda took a few swigs and felt less nervous. By the time the joint came to her, she was already drunk, and it seemed like a good idea. She puffed on the joint and tried to ignore the burning in her chest.

Margie dragged Matt to standing. "We'll be back later! Don't do anything we wouldn't do." They disappeared into another part of the house.

The room began to move around Amanda like water, the curtains rippling in the pulsing half-light. The drumbeat through the stereo speakers thumped in her gut. Nausea. She put her hands over her face. "Can you turn it down?"

The music changed to something slow and quiet. "Hey." Kenneth was right beside her. "Is that better?"

He pulled her hands away from her face and stared into her eyes. "Do you remember how we used to play in the park?" For a moment, Amanda thought he wanted to kiss her, but instead, he encircled her wrists with his blunt fingers and pushed back hard against her shoulders. She fell backward easily, her limbs soft and leaden. Then he got on top of her, and she began to sink under his body.

"What are you doing?" The words slid from her mouth, unintelligible.

He tugged at her jeans. Her hips became a distant and unmanageable part of her body. She jerked awkwardly as he pulled at her clothes until she felt his full weight pressed against her chest. Then the tops of her thighs were bare. She turned her head to the side, desperate not to vomit, and stared at the black hole of night through the uncovered window.

A door slammed. Footsteps. Voices from outside.

"Just relax," Kenneth said, in a low growl, forced between his teeth. His nails scraped against her skin as he grabbed at and yanked down her underwear with one hand. The elastic cut into her and burned until the underwear finally ripped and loosened. "Yeah, I know who you are."

"Is this what it is? Is it this?" Amanda burbled. Then clearly, urgently, to the blank-faced sky outside. "Is this what you meant for me?"

She struggled to lift her head, but the boy pushed heavily on her forehead and held her down. Amanda squeezed her eyes shut, stopped her breath. She went under.

The music hissed and glistened behind a rhythmic clunking on the floor beside her, heavy and methodical for a while, then sped up, frantic. Then it stopped.

Amanda came back to the surface and gasped for air. The pressure on her body lifted, and for a moment she had the sensation of floating upward. Kenneth rolled off her and sat up against the sofa. He locked his heavy belt buckle back in place, reached for the tequila bottle and took a swig, wiped his mouth against his forearm. "I knew you'd like it." He grinned meanly and showed his very white, straight teeth. "Are you happy now?"

Amanda wobbled to her feet and grabbed at her clothes, trying to pull them all up at once. She pushed her damp hair back off her face. "Where's Margie?"

"Don't bother with her." Kenneth put his head back, closed his eyes and breathed deeply, easily.

Amanda stood in the middle of the living room, gripping the waistband of her undone jeans. Her head spun. She froze in place, not sure where to go next, or even how to step forward without falling. Pain began to bloom inside her. She reached down and felt the cold wetness between her thighs. Was it blood?

What was she doing here? She was supposed to be somewhere else. She gazed slowly around the room, followed the low light that spilled from the kitchen. A cup sat on the small, round dining table, and one of the chairs had been pushed back as if someone had just got up. There was an empty dish rack on the counter, dirty dishes beside the sink. A kettle. A tea towel had been neatly folded and hung over the handle of the stove. A kitchen – familiar, but it looked fake, like a museum reconstruction.

The music ended. The boy's snoring buzzed.

A red glow appeared in the window, flared for a moment, dimmed again. Flared and dimmed like a lighthouse signal. Amanda took a step forward and found she was steady enough to move toward it. She put her forehead against the cool glass and looked out.

Outside, Margie stood on the porch, Matt in front of her on a plastic chair. Margie's dress, luminous in the moonlight, fluttered and lifted.

Amanda held her breath.

The moon slipped behind a cloud. Margie dragged on her cigarette, then said something to Matt, took another drag, then flicked her cigarette away. Its light arced in the darkness then disappeared. She sat on the boy's knee, and they began to kiss.

Amanda turned and stared at Kenneth, on the couch. Asleep, he looked more like the little motherless boy she remembered.

"Was it supposed to happen?" She looked up. Listened. "Or was it my fault?"

Kenneth sighed and shifted. His head fell and nodded against his shoulder.

CHICKEN

Mimi's in the shower with the curtain open when Fiona goes into the bathroom to brush her teeth before school. Mimi always takes too long on her day off and makes Fiona late – one more late slip and she'll have to stay for detention, and Margie and Kenneth will walk to the skate park without her. But Mimi couldn't care less. She holds her hands up over her head and turns side to side to catch a glimpse of herself in the steamy bathroom mirror. "Take a look at this, Fi." Her boobs are covered in deep-purple egg-shaped bruises. "What do you think?"

Fiona stares with her mouth wide open, drooling toothpaste. Mimi laughs and lifts one breast with each hand and looks down. Soap foam slides off the tips of her nipples. "John did that."

Fiona spits in the sink and gulps some water out of the tap. "Gross," she says. "That's filthy." She's seen hickeys before, who hasn't? But only on necks. Fiona slams the door on the way out and immediately the shower turns off.

"Fi! Fiona! Come back!"

At least she's wrapped in a towel when Fiona returns. "What now?"

"John's coming over tonight. Said he makes the best roast chicken." Mimi's towel has fallen away completely. Slowly, she circles her hands around her breasts, backward and forward. "Mmm, I love roast chicken."

"You're disgusting."

"When was the last time Mum managed to make dinner?"

"You're naked and covered in sex bruises and salivating over your boyfriend and his roast chicken and you work in a *chicken factory*. Yuck." No one is even allowed near the building except the workers, so Fiona doesn't know what it's like for sure, but Mimi has stories. She says the stench of chlorine and blood and chicken shit would just knock you out, if you weren't used to it. She says she stands in a pool of blood mixed with chicken fat and water and chemicals in the freezing cold while she slices the spindly wings off the chickens, right at the shoulder, one after another, all day long. She says when you look around sometimes, you might think that every single person there was bleeding to death because everyone has a knife in their hand and a puddle of blood at their feet. And she laughs at that every time she says it because she thinks it's funny.

Mimi met John at the plant. The day Mimi started he said, "Why are you working here? Did you just get out of prison?" She told Fiona she didn't get it until John explained later it was because she was white.

"But isn't he white?" Fiona said. "Did you ask him?"

"What? Did I ask him what?"

"Did you ask him if he just got out of prison?"

"Why would I ask him that?"

"Because he's white."

"He's the *foreman*?" she said, as though it explained everything.

Mimi had started working at the chicken factory right after she barely finished high school, nearly four years ago. John Clark had arrived at the plant six weeks earlier, freshly divorced. "New start," he said, which included Mimi, apparently.

"It's not like I have a choice," she said, when Fiona called her an idiot for interviewing there in the first place. "There's nothing else and Mum can't make any money." Still, Fiona wonders now: Does Mimi have to fuck the foreman? Does she have to eat the chicken?

·   ·   ·

By the time Fiona gets to school, Principal Sumich is hanging around the office to stalk latecomers and give them fatherly advice. "That's ten lates this month, Fiona. You know you can do better. You can do well. You have potential." He tells Fiona to go to 5A for detention right after the final bell. "It's for your own good. You'll thank me one day."

"What happens if I don't go?"

He folds his arms and sighs, the way teachers do. "Then you'll get a suspension."

"And then what?"

"It will go on your record."

"And?"

"Well." He's flustered, and Fiona is ecstatic for a few seconds. "Why don't you take this seriously? This is your future we're talking about right here."

Fiona laughs in his face. "What future?"

"You're smart, Fiona. You can have a good life, if you want one. But you have to want it."

"So, it's all up to me?"

He nods his head, glad she's finally figured it out.

"Well, sir. I guess I just don't understand. Why did you want to be the principal of a shithole high school?"

"Get to class," he snaps.

"Hey, skinny," Kenneth says when he meets up with Fiona and Margie after school, but he doesn't take his eyes off Margie. Margie tells Fiona that when Kenneth calls her skinny it's a good thing, like she's a model. But Fiona's five foot two, and Margie knows, and Fiona knows too, that what Kenneth means is she looks like she's in eighth grade, not twelfth. She doesn't have any of Mimi's curves. No breasts. She's all bones and skin.

The girls smoke cigarettes and watch Kenneth skateboarding until he's done flipping his board all over the concrete. When he finally sits down on the grass with a joint, Fiona says, "You'll never guess what my sister showed me this morning."

"Holy shit, your sister is hot." He makes fake boobs with his hands above his own chest.

"What did she show you?" Margie says.

"So hot." He grins, eyes half-closed, smoke pouring from his open mouth.

"Come on! Is it nasty?"

"It's nothing. Whatever. She's not hot, anyway. She stinks like dead chicken and has to shower twice a day."

"Your sister in the shower!" Kenneth licks his lips.

Fiona decides to not even tell them about Mimi's boob bruises now. Like Sumich said, she's smart.

Mimi has Fridays off instead of Saturdays. The plant gets shut down on Sunday, but they keep it running the other six days, so no one gets a weekend. Mimi says if the workers had two days off in a row they would never go back to work after the second day. She says if you had two in a row, you'd spend the second day thinking about how incredibly shitty your life was, and that would be it, you'd shove your head in the electrocution bath and knock your own self senseless along with the chickens. She's bone-tired all the time, but she doesn't sleep on her day off. She lies on the sofa and watches soaps all afternoon until their mother, Deb, gets up, just after Fiona gets home from school.

"Roast chicken!" Mimi yells as soon as Fiona walks in, like it's Christmas.

"I'm not going to eat it."

"It would be rude not to."

"Rude. As if anyone around here cares."

"Chicken?" Deb is at the living room door in the pink chenille dressing gown she wears every single day. Big patches of the fluff have worn down, so it looks like she's wrapped herself up in a sheet of balding skin. "I need a cuppa," she croaks, then takes a deep drag on her first smoke of the day, her favourite.

"John's coming," Mimi says. "He's cooking dinner."

"Oh." Deb looks confused. "Do I have to get dressed?" Then immediately, "I should get dressed. When's he coming?"

Deb has papered the walls of their bungalow with inspirational posters that have pictures of kittens and sunsets and say things like, "Don't count the days, make the days count," and "Shoot for the moon – even if you miss, you'll land among the stars," and "Life begins at the end of your comfort zone." For the past eight years, ever since she kicked the girls' dad out for good, she has had depression-induced insomnia.

"Don't worry about it, Mum," Mimi says. "It's just John. He wants to do something nice for us."

Fiona has only met John once, a couple of weeks after Mimi started going out with him. He gave Mimi a lift home and said hi and waved to Fiona when Mimi got out of the car. He wore a short-sleeved business shirt and a too-wide tie. He had hairy arms but was thinning on top of his head. He looked like someone's dad, which wasn't surprising to Fiona because he had two young children, now in the custody of his wife.

"He must be a very nice man." Deb's face is pinched, as if she's still got her cigarette in her mouth, even though it's dangling from her fingers.

"Very nice." Mimi shifts her bra underwire to lift her bust and smirks at Fiona, who makes Deb's coffee and tries not to think about Mimi's breasts.

•　•　•

John arrives with two chickens about the time Deb is putting on her makeup for the first time – the time before she starts to cry and has to start again. "Hello, ladies," he booms when he bursts through the back door without knocking. He stands with his arms open wide, like Jesus on the cross, a plastic-bag-covered chicken in each hand dripping watery blood on the floor. "Look what I bought for you!"

"Big deal. You're a foreman at the chicken plant," Fiona says. "Did you even have to pay for them?"

He just stretches his arms wider, causing his beer gut to dislodge his shirt from his pants and expose his pasty middle. He's still holding the chickens when Mimi wraps her arms around his neck and sticks her tongue in his mouth. Fiona doesn't know how long they keep up with that because she leaves right away to find out if her mum is ready.

Deb's in her dressing gown again, pulling the venetian blinds shut in her bedroom. It's still light outside. The clothes she was wearing are in a pile on the floor. "Migraine," she whispers, squinting. She creeps over to her bed and lies down flat on her back.

Her bedside transistor radio crackles. Static and talkback are her constant soundtrack in here. Fiona stares at the poster above her head that reads "It does not matter how slowly you go as long as you do not stop," and tries not to get mad. It occurs to her for about the thousandth time that it's the only poster Deb pays attention to, and she takes it too literally, and maybe Fiona should just pull it off the wall.

"So, you're not coming? You're going to leave me alone with them?"

Deb's eyelids flutter closed. "Don't talk so loudly. It hurts. I need –"

"I know."

· · ·

"Really?" Mimi says when she sees Fiona open the freezer door. "Again?"

John is tying string around one of the chicken's ankles. The chicken is greasy and as fat and pale pink as a newborn baby. The sight of the string tied so tightly around the bottom of its footless legs makes Fiona want to cry. "What's going on?" he says. "Can I do anything?"

Fiona takes out the morphine suppositories from way in the back of the freezer. Deb can't swallow morphine. It makes her vomit.

She sneaks into the dim room and leaves the drugs on the bedside table. Deb has a washcloth over her eyes now, to keep all the light out, and she lies rigid on the bed, vigilant, as if relaxing would invite the pain to stay longer. She reaches for the bottle, and Fiona creeps out. She would stay, soothe her, somehow, but it wouldn't do any good. Neither Fiona or Mimi exist when Deb's like this.

For the next hour, Fiona sits in her bedroom and watches TV and tries to ignore the sound of her mum's sobbing coming through the walls until Mimi yells, "Dinner!"

The kitchen is a mess from one end to the other, the sink piled high with dirty dishes. "You can clean up after we eat," Mimi says in the fake nice voice she uses when she's pretending to be the grown-up in charge, "since John made the food."

"Why me? What about you?"

"I have to entertain John."

Fiona follows her as she carries two plates to the dining table. The magazines, pens, mail and all the other junk that's usually all over the table have been moved to a neat stack at one end, and John is already at the table with a plate, gnawing a chicken drumstick. When he notices the girls, he stops eating for a minute and gestures to the chairs. "Take a seat," he says, as though it's his house.

Mimi puts one of the plates down in front of Fiona and Fiona pokes at the flesh with her fork. "It looks stringy."

John snorts, his mouth full of food.

She pushes the plate away. "It stinks."

"You never eat anything," Mimi says. "Your elbows stick out. There's such a thing as too skinny, you know." When she starts to eat, she makes faces at John that Fiona thinks she probably imagines are sexy while she chews up the dead bird. "Mmm. It's so good, honey."

"Nothing like home cooking," John says, and nudges Fiona's plate back. "Right, Fiona?" He nods his head slowly, as though they agree. "Look at us here, like a little family." He starts to ask Fiona questions about school and what movies and music she likes and all the other sorts of questions adults ask when they don't know what to say.

Mimi's annoyed because John's not paying any attention to her, so Fiona eggs him on and makes up lies to all his questions while she cuts the chicken into tiny pieces and pushes it around without taking a bite.

"Do you have a boyfriend?" He attacks the limb in his hand noisily, sucking off all the flesh and fat, then drops the clean bone on his plate.

"Oh. Well, I probably shouldn't tell you this, but I'm having an affair with my principal. His wife just doesn't understand him, and we have so much in common."

"I bet you do!" John hoots. "Sounds a lot like my ex." He winks at her.

"She is not." Mimi pouts. "Obviously."

"What are you going to do once you finish school?" John says.

"When I grow up? Let's see. I'm thinking of becoming an astronaut. Or maybe I'll lecture in experimental physics somewhere in the States. Or I'll go the artistic route – sculpture, or art film. Maybe I'll just travel around Europe, you know, taking photos."

"I can get you a job at the plant," he says, serious now.

"Thanks. I'm pretty sure I could get myself a job at the plant. You don't exactly have to be a genius."

"Well, I kinda doubt you're a genius." He laughs his head off at that, and so does Mimi. "How old are you, anyway?"

"Seventeen."

He makes a face, confused, maybe even disappointed. "I thought you were younger."

"Everybody does," Mimi says. "Because she's so tiny and flat." She tears a strip of meat with her fingers and nibbles it with her front teeth.

Fiona remembers about her boobs again and can hardly even look at John. She starts clearing their bone-covered plates and her own, still full of all the food she won't eat, the chicken breast now cold and limp, the fat congealed beneath it a glassy, beige jelly.

She starts to clean up in the kitchen, but after five minutes, Mimi calls out, "Fi, come in here. You've gotta see these."

Mimi is snuggled up to John on the sofa, and they're looking through their mum's old photo albums. John has his hand on a page to stop Mimi from turning it, even though she tugs on the corner. "Wait," he says, then turns to Fiona. "Costume party? Who are you supposed to be?"

Fiona is eleven years old and wearing a fake leopard-skin bikini top and a ragged denim miniskirt, her pale, chubby middle rolling over the waistband, and she has a half-ponytail on the top of her head with a bleached chicken drumstick bone through it. She's sitting on the grass, leaning back with her hand behind her head and one knee bent up. A pin-up pose she must have seen somewhere. She tries to imagine what her mother was thinking when she let her pose like that for the photo.

"Who do you think?" Fiona says. But he just shakes his head. "Pebbles. From *The Flintstones*? It's this old cartoon Dad used to let us watch."

"Oh yeah. I remember that," Mimi says. "Nice bikini top, Fi. Your baby fat looks super sexy." Fiona knows Mimi means she looks stupid.

John stares hard at the photo, bringing his face closer, until Mimi finally gets control of the album and turns the page.

"I killed a chicken myself once," Fiona says. "Margie and I got into her neighbour's coop when her neighbour was out. We wanted to see if there were any eggs. We were just kids, and there were no eggs anyway. But one of the chickens got out of the coop and started running around the yard, over the dry grass and the cracked path, clucking like crazy. We knew if we didn't get the chicken back in the coop we'd be in trouble because Margie's neighbour hated kids, especially Margie, and she'd tell Margie's dad, and then he would beat the shit out of her because that's what he does. And so, when this chicken started running around the yard, we thought the best way to get it back in the coop would be to corner it and grab it in our hands, but we kept missing it, and then it ran straight for the open gate at the back of the yard, and we realized at the same time that if it got out and into the laneway and onto the road we would both be in serious trouble. Margie yelled, 'Fi! Get the gate!' So instead of just letting it go, I ran for the gate. But I didn't quite make it in time, and just as I slammed it shut, the chicken stuck its neck out like it was trying to win a race or something, and I chopped the chicken's head clean off. That was bad enough, but worse, the headless body just kept running around the yard for a while until it fell over, its feet scratching in the air. There was blood everywhere, and Margie and I were both screaming and bawling. The neighbour came yelling to our parents. Margie's dad gave her a walloping, and Mum was so embarrassed she didn't talk to me for a week. Remember that?"

Mimi frowns at Fiona. "No."

John has been hanging on her every word. He laughs loudly and slaps his thigh.

"Dad would have laughed about it too, but he was already gone." She looks away. Whispers, "I still have nightmares about that chicken. Sometimes I think that chicken is Dad. Sometimes it's Mum. Sometimes, I think it's me."

"Why are you so weird?" Mimi slams the album shut.

Later, after Mimi and John have gone out somewhere, Fiona finds the album on the coffee table. She sits and takes a look through it, even at the earliest pages that Mimi avoided, the ones where their mother is in a dress with her hair up. The ones with their dad in them. But when she gets to the page that should have the photo of her as Pebbles, it's not there.

The next morning when Fiona gets up, John's in Mimi's short red satin robe and a pair of athletic socks, drinking coffee on the sofa in the living room. Just sitting, facing the door, like he's waiting for something. The photo of Fiona from the album is on the coffee table in front of him.

"I didn't know you were staying over." Fiona wishes she wasn't only wearing a tank top and underwear. John stares at her naked legs and goosebumps rise on her skin.

"It's our day off." His voice doesn't fill up the space for once. He purrs, almost. "Don't you think it's like I'm part of the family now?"

"Does Mum know you're here?"

"We played checkers late last night, after you were asleep. The three of us. Mimi's no good, of course. You should have stayed up.

I bet you're good at it." His eyes flick over her body. "You're smart. I can tell."

She tugs at the hem of her T-shirt. "I hate checkers."

"Do you want me to make you some breakfast?" he says, as though Fiona is the visitor.

"I don't eat breakfast."

"You don't eat anything. Your mother must be worried about you."

"I'm going back to bed."

"Can I come?"

She thinks she has misheard him, but isn't sure, and stands frozen.

She takes a step backward. "Where's Mimi?"

"Fast asleep." He smiles, eyes half-closed. "She's exhausted. You know why." He shifts in his seat until the robe falls open, and Fiona can see that he's hard.

Fiona slides the lock Deb put on her bedroom door when their dad was still living there, then goes back to bed and sleeps all day, on and off, her clock radio on low. When she wakes up around half past three, it occurs to her that her mum is onto something, but not long after that, Deb bangs on the door. "Fiona! Get up. You can't stay in bed all day."

As soon as she cracks her bedroom door, Fiona hears the rattle of dice and John's rumble from the dining room, his voice big again.

John, Mimi and Deb are at the table playing Monopoly, the board and the money taking up most of the tabletop. Deb is dressed in the clothes she used to wear to work – makeup, too, and her perfect, oval nails have been freshly painted, deep pink. She lights the end of a new cigarette with the burning end of the one she's just finishing. When the cigarette is lit, she squashes the other in the ashtray, then drapes one arm over the back of her chair, stretches her legs out and raises her cigarette, expertly balanced between her slender fingers, to her lips. She takes a drag, one eye half-closed, then blows the smoke upward in a thin stream. She looks elegant, like something out of a movie.

"We've only just started," she says when she sees Fiona. "Sit down on that end."

Mimi leans on the edge of the table toward John, her arms folded underneath her boobs to push them up, but he ignores her and counts his money. He says, "Don't you wish this money was real?" as if no one had ever said that before, and Deb laughs, as if it's the funniest thing she ever heard.

"I don't want to play."

"Sure you do," John says. He shuffles his chair sideways to make room beside him. "Of course you do."

Mimi pulls at the collar of her T-shirt. There are new bruises, higher up. Then she grabs Deb's box of smokes, shakes one out and lights it, presses her lips together hard over the filter.

"Mercy!" Which is what Deb calls Mimi when Mimi's in trouble.

"Mum, I'm a grown woman now!" Mimi puts her elbow on the table and tries to balance the cigarette, but her hand shakes violently and she drops the smoke. "Shit. My RSI. All those hours slicing wings off in the freezing cold." She opens and closes her fist, wincing.

"I don't think so." John picks up the cigarette, takes a drag. He already has seven properties on the board.

"You don't know what it's like." Mimi massages her arm.

"I think I do."

"Whatever. I don't want to play. I'm so bored. I need to get out of here." Mimi stands, one hand on her hip, and waits for John to get up too.

"Mercy," Deb says again, but not mad this time. She doesn't want Mimi to leave. Playing board games is the only thing they ever do together. Mimi flounces out anyway, all huffy.

"Well," Deb says, dragging herself to her feet. "I'll go and see if I can convince her."

"I'll get her, Mum."

John presses down on Fiona's shoulder when she starts to get up. "No. Let your mother."

"You know how she gets." Deb shuffles out of the room, her momentary brightness already dimmed by the first sign of conflict.

John looks up from counting his money and smiles at Fiona. "Sure do, Deb."

Fiona's mother has barely left when John slaps his other hand down on Fiona's leg and begins to squeeze and knead the muscle above her knee. "Just us."

"Mum?" Fiona stares at her thigh, but it no longer seems connected to her body. She can see his hand, squeezing, but can't feel it.

"Don't make trouble for your mother. Hasn't she got enough to worry about? And Mimi working so hard while you hang out with your friends. You've got it easy." He lets go of Fiona's leg, snakes his arm around the back of her neck and pushes her face toward his. "How about a kiss?"

In the hallway, Deb is knocking on Mimi's door with short, insistent taps. "Family time," she says. "Mimi. It'll be fun. Come on now. Like it used to be."

John grabs Fiona's jaw and kisses her. His tongue probing her mouth, his teeth pinching her top lip. He puts his palm flat against her chest, makes frantic circles. Fiona slumps in her chair, boneless, stares at the tiny folds in his eyelids, focuses on the knocking in the background. Matches it with her heartbeat.

· · ·

Later, alone with Deb in her dark room, Fiona tells her she doesn't want to be alone with John again.

Deb startles. "What?" she says. "Why?"

"He touched me." She says this hushed, so Mimi can't hear. Low, in the background, on the radio, in a way that sounds like water running down a drain, someone is saying, "Well, who's to blame, who's to blame for that? I mean, come on, mate, who's to blame? They're always complaining, complaining about this and that and every gee-dee thing. But whose fault is it, mate? You tell me, huh?"

Fiona holds her breath and wonders if her mother will move fast enough to save her this time.

Deb sits on the edge of her bed with her eyes squeezed shut, as though if she can't see Fiona anymore, she won't exist. She sighs heavily, gets into bed in slow motion, buries herself under the covers and makes circles on either side of her forehead with her fingertips. She looks at Fiona at last, wounded. "Just stay out of his way. What would we do if Mimi lost her job?"

"Hurry up, Fi," Mimi says. Fiona has beaten her to the shower for once. She wants to leave early and get to school on time. They have exams soon. There's not much time left. Mimi pulls back the curtain, and Fiona rips it back into place. "Your ribs! Your bones," Mimi says. "Holy shit. You look like you weigh five stone!"

The water drums hard. "Get out!" Fiona turns up the heat and the steam rises.

"Things are going to get better around here," Mimi yells above the shower. "You'll see. John's moving in. He wants to help us out."

Fiona gets out of the shower and wraps herself in a towel as quickly as possible. "He can't! He's your boss."

Mimi easily circles Fiona's wrist with her forefinger and thumb.

"Mum's more like her old self when John's around. Like when Dad was here." She rattles Fiona's arm up and down and it flaps awkwardly, like a broken wing. "You need to eat something," she says gently. "Who's going to want you like that? Men like a bit of meat."

When Fiona gets home from school, Mimi and John are at the table, facing each other, eating cold chicken with their hands, lips slick with grease. "John got you a job at the plant," Mimi says, excited. "You can start next week."

"You can thank me later," John says, then returns to sucking a bare bone, looking at Fiona while he slides his tongue along it.

"You're lucky. They're on a hiring freeze, but John pulled some strings."

"I haven't even finished school yet."

"What the point?" John says.

"I'm going to finish. Then . . ." But she doesn't know. She doesn't know what happens next.

John leans back, hands across his belly, and smiles at her over the pile of bones.

There's no way out.

Suddenly, Fiona is dizzy with hunger for the first time in months. She snatches an entire breast off Mimi's plate, rips it apart with her fingers and bites at the meat frantically, shoving it into her mouth, swallowing without chewing.

"Fi!" Mimi says. "Slow down."

The world disappears. Her hunger yawns inside her, an unfillable hole. She can't eat fast enough. She bites so hard, she chews through her own tongue and her mouth fills with blood. She can barely breathe as she gulps it all down.

"Fiona!" Mimi tries to take hold of her hands, but Fiona flutters out of reach.

John stands up behind her and pulls back roughly on her upper arms until she feels a tearing at her shoulders. "Stop it!" he barks.

But it's too late. He can't catch her. She crunches through the brittle bones beneath the breast meat and the splinters lodge in her throat.

RUBBER

Already, at ten to nine, there's this woman banging on the front doors. Then she stops banging to peer in with her hands cupped around her eyes and tries to see if there's anyone here yet. We're not supposed to open until nine, but Liz opens the doors anyway. "Good morning – welcome!" she says to the woman, like we're on TV, and she's the worst host of the worst game show ever made.

The woman's in slippers, a kitten-and-glitter-covered T-shirt with no bra, by the looks of it, and a pair of burgundy sweatpants – everything plus-plus-sized, but still a size too small. A roll of fat, smooth and pink as luncheon meat, billows from underneath the hem of her shirt. The woman doesn't say good morning back, just flicks her cigarette on the concrete step without bothering to put it out – maybe she doesn't want her slippers to catch fire, or more likely she's just lazy – then she pushes right past Liz and goes over to the sneaker display on the wall. Liz fake-smiles as the woman passes, then props up the Open sign on the sidewalk.

After she comes back in, Liz straightens the mat, picks up and rehangs a coat and jabs some flip-flops back into place on the rack. She doesn't stop. If you couldn't see her expression while she tidied up, you would think she liked this job.

Liz tells me that I have to polish the counter before anybody gets here. There's already someone here, but that doesn't seem to make a difference to Liz. Once she's hooked the doors back to show we are well and truly open, she comes over to the register and watches to make sure I polish properly, as though I'm a total moron and can't clean a countertop. I rub hard in big circles and say, "Wax on, wax off." It's funny, but it just seems to annoy her. I bet she never goes to the movies or does anything fun, so she probably doesn't get it.

The smell of the cleaner makes me gag, but there's no way I want Liz to know that, so as soon as she goes to unpack boxes in the stockroom, I stop wiping.

By then, Mrs. Sweatpants is busy pulling all the sneakers off the shelves and checking the shoe sizes, even though I spent hours yesterday afternoon matching the shoes and making sure all the fives went with the fives and the sixes with the sixes – and all the rest of them, right up to eleven. Women's, men's and kids'. That's a lot of sneakers to organize. By one minute to nine, there's a pile of shoes on the floor beside her, sizes all mixed up. Finally, she sits herself down on the padded bench and squeezes a swollen purple foot into a pair of bright-white plastic sneakers with an extra-thick sole. She bends over, pulls back on the laces and wheezes. She has to strain to get the shoes on because she's got a lot of gut to get past.

"Margie! Go and help her," Liz says from the stockroom door to the back of my head. I think about saying, "I thought I was cleaning the countertop, Liz, what are *you* doing?" But I'm not stupid. Instead, I put the cloth and spray bottle beneath the cash register and walk as slowly as I can over to the woman. By the time I reach her, she is actually panting with the effort of doing up the goddamn shoelace.

When she sees me coming, the woman lets go of the laces, leans back in the chair and just waits for me to get down and crouch over her foot and do the laces up for her, like she's the Queen. I finally get the shoe done up and say, "How does that feel, ma'am?" even though I couldn't care less.

"Hmm." She cranes her head over her stomach to get an eyeful of her foot, bends her ankle right and left. "Why aren't they on sale?" Considering her size, her voice is surprisingly high-pitched. It sort of lilts, like music. It's pretty.

The blood rushes to my head when I stand, and I have to put my hand on the rack to steady myself. It's tiring just standing up lately. "Ma'am, unfortunately, these sneakers are full price right now. Probably they'll go on sale later, but they're from our new line." I have to smile at this point; it's called *customer service*.

"There won't be any of my size left then. I have a common size." Then she just sits there. She barely managed to get dressed this morning, but she's smeared her eyelids with creamy, baby-blue eyeshadow, like she's a teenager and it's still the '70s. Maybe she's got a hot date.

"Ma'am," I say again, because Liz told me last week that if I didn't start saying "ma'am" she'd tell head office, "maybe you could try on another style that isn't so expensive." To tell the truth, there's not much chance of that, because all the shoes in here are cheap, especially the ones she's squashed her feet into. It's hard to get cheaper than that.

I wave my hand vaguely toward the end of the shelves where we've displayed the thin-soled, cloth sneakers from the end of summer. Liz ordered way too many and told me put them on the end of the aisle to get people's attention, but no one's fooled. Liz keeps bugging me to sell them anyway. "Make a sale," she says. "Make an effort for once."

I just say, "Commission?" She knows as well as I do, we don't get any, and that's the end of that.

Instead of answering me, the woman huffs and puffs and hems and haws, rotates her left foot slowly, pushes up onto her toes. "They fit okay, I guess." This doesn't make her happy though. She sighs and slumps back in her chair.

"Ma'am, why don't you think about it for a while?"

As I walk away, she says, "Well," in that baby voice, and I have the thought that I could help her, but it's past nine and other customers are coming through the doors, so I pretend that I'm too busy and don't turn around.

Liz is standing at the counter with her arms folded, squinting through her plastic, square-rimmed glasses at her fingernails. She takes great pride in her nails and files them into polished claws every lunchtime after she's gulped down her daily ham sandwich – the loaf kind of ham, you can tell, because the square edges of the meat poke outside the bread crusts. She sits in our beige fluorescent lunchroom all by herself and reads her *Woman's Weekly*, cover to cover. She tells me she's too tired to go anywhere, but I know it's really because she likes to spy on me and make sure that even if there is absolutely nothing left to do, that I am doing something.

After staring at her nails, Liz pats down her hair. She goes on and on about her curly hair, how her mother had curly hair too. But it's not natural. It's so tight and frizzy, it looks crunchy. It's obviously a perm. A home perm – there's no way she has the money for a salon one, working here, where all we sell are things made out of rubber. Really! Rubber things, and plasticky fake rubber, like the shoes. Liz told me once that the shoes were just a branching-out from the rubber boots and hoses the store carried originally. After that the store got so popular it became a chain. Can you believe it? The history of this place is fascinating.

I start spraying and polishing, and I guess because she's also bored already, or maybe because she just likes telling me what to do, Liz hisses at me, "Fold your collar down." Then she tugs at it herself, like she's my mother, though my mother wouldn't give a damn what I wore. "And take those earrings out of your ears." I can't really blame her. If I looked like she did, I would try and make me worse-looking too – although, to be honest, I'm already pretty ugly at work, even when I get away with wearing jewellery, because if the stinking rubber weren't bad enough, there's the uni-form I have to wear. It's a kind of long, light brown shirtdress with a brown-and-white–checked collar and dark brown plastic buttons all the way down the front, from my chest to just below my knees where the dress stops – a length that makes even my calves look fat. My friend Amanda says I remind her of a psychiatric nurse when I wear it, which is fitting, if you think about what I put up with every day. Most days, I pop the top button open and wear it that way until Liz ogles my cleavage and tells me to do it back up. I didn't pop it today though. She might notice my boobs are getting bigger.

I should be helping our new customers because Liz doesn't seem to be bothering, but I pretend to clean because I would rather feel sick than have to talk to anyone else. For a while I watch a shrivelled old man run his crooked fingers through the rubber O-rings with intense concentration, until I'm distracted by a commotion near the raincoats.

A woman who isn't much older than I am is trying to keep her snotty toddler still long enough to shove him into a ladybug raincoat, which is clearly supposed to be for a girl. Once the mother has wrestled the toddler's arms into the coat, the kid starts shrieking and kicking up a fuss, and his mother gets mad and counts to three, slow and low, but it doesn't make the slightest bit of difference. Then the kid starts screaming, drops to the floor and rolls around on the carpet until he goes red in the face. Bright red, nearly purple. Lint gets stuck all over the coat before the kid rips it off, throws it in a heap and stomps up and down on it. It's probably damaged, but his mother doesn't pay any attention to the coat. She tries to take hold of him but gets smacked by the kid's flailing arms and legs. She yells, "Stop this behaviour right now!" He totally ignores her and screams louder. I never would have done that when I was a kid – my dad's too quick with his fists, and I'm a fast learner.

"See? That's what it's like." Liz has crept out of the stockroom. She glares at me. "It's no picnic, let me tell you. Especially when you're on your own."

"But babies are adorable, don't you think?"

"They don't stay babies for long. And you have no idea how

they're going to turn out. It doesn't matter what you do. And then you'll blame yourself, no matter what."

The mother digs a bar of chocolate out of her handbag and shakes it in her kid's face. This finally gets the toddler's attention and keeps him quiet enough for the mother to stuff him in his crappy umbrella stroller and tighten the straps so he can't get out. We don't like it when customers eat in the store, but even Liz doesn't say anything about the chocolate this time. The mother hangs the coat back up, all crooked, and doesn't even bother to snap the buttons back together before they leave.

By then, Mrs. Sweatpants is trying on another pair of shoes, light blue this time, like her eyeshadow. It must be her favourite colour. These shoes fasten with Velcro, like children's shoes, but they go all the way up to men's size eleven. It seems she can manage the Velcro by herself, thankfully. She makes a little grunt, and then they're all done up. Next, she pushes up from the chair and admires herself in the full-length mirror that hangs on the wall beside the raincoats.

She turns her feet side to side, scrunches up her nose and pulls up the bottom of her sweatpants past her ankles, so she can see her feet better. It must be obvious even to her that the shoes are terrible, but because no one in their right mind would want to actually wear them in public, these ones are on sale.

"I hope she doesn't want a ladybug raincoat to go with those shoes," I whisper to Liz. "I think we're out of her size." Liz doesn't find it funny, just tells me to stop wasting time and points one of her claws at the countertop I've already wiped approximately sixty thousand times since we opened.

Still at the mirror, Mrs. Glitter-Kittens swivels her head around and opens her mouth, hoping to get our attention, but at the same time a man wearing "The Executive," one of our beige trench coats from last season, tiptoes up to the counter. I know what he wants before he asks for it. You just get a sense for these things – and of course, there's the trench coat; it's not exactly original. "I was wondering," he says in a fake posh voice. That's it. Then he just stands there for about half an hour staring at my straining top button, his hands deep in the coat pockets. He only snaps back into action because I sigh loudly. He leans in and whispers, "I was wondering, miss, if you sell rubber sheets." He's so close, I can see the foamy spit in the corners of his mouth, the yellow crust where his eyes meet the bridge of his nose.

They always think I'm going to say no; I swear. Maybe they think I'll shriek and wet myself. But when I lean in closer and whisper back, "Sure we do," because we do, he says he'll come back later and scuttles away.

Liz is in the office. I can see her through the sliding glass window that lets her see out into the shop. She's on the phone and wants me to think she's calling in the order to the warehouse because the order book is out on the table. But we haven't counted the stock yet and have no idea what we need. I know she's called Matt, anyway, because she's gripping the phone handle hard with both hands, and you can see in her face and in the way the tendons in her neck pop out that she's yelling her head off, only really quietly. That's how she always speaks to Matt. He's her pride and joy . . . not. Nineteen and unemployed and not in university either. He's categorically a loser, but sexy as hell. Maybe Liz thinks it's her fault that Matt's the way he is, and that's why she's so crabby all the time.

When Liz notices me, she flicks her fingers and waves the back of her hand toward the woman who is treading around in the blue shoes. Instead, I cross back and stand in the stockroom because it connects to the office. The door is partly open, and, from there, Liz can't see me, but I can hear every word she says.

"Again? . . . I don't have any money . . . What will you . . . ? What? No." Silence. "Are you sure it's yours?" Then "Oh my God.

You can't –" Then "Will you tell me who it is?" She's not pleading, not even angry, she just sounds defeated. I guess Matt doesn't tell her what she wants to know because almost straightaway she slams the phone down in the cradle, then puts her face in her hands. I get out of there before she catches me listening.

Once I'm back on the shop floor, I take my time and wander back over to Mrs. Sweatpants. Apparently, she's decided not to buy anything because she's taken off the blue sneakers and has scrunched her feet back into her fluffy slippers, and when I reach her, she tries to avoid me and gathers up her tatty, peeling handbag and plastic shopping bag.

At this point, the employee manual tells me, I should try to keep the customer in the store and encourage them to buy one of the items they had been considering. Close the deal. What the employee handbook doesn't account for is what happens when this particular customer wants to make it clear to me she's finished and won't be buying anything at all, thank you very much, no doubt to avoid my high-pressure sales tactics. Flustered and in a hurry, she stands and attempts to put the shoes she's been trying on back on the rack where they belong, but in her eagerness to get out of there, she knocks the rack over. I mean, the whole thing. All the shelving collapses, and all the shoes go flying and get mixed up with each other. Almost every kind of shoe we sell is white. It's literally an avalanche.

Even though she must be pretty old, Liz can move at lightning speed, like a snake, or maybe a crocodile, if you want a really good comparison, and she appears suddenly from the office and zips right there before the woman or I have even had a chance to react.

Mrs. Sweatpants and I both just stand there gaping at the disaster, but Liz throws her arms wide and yells, "What have you done?" At first, I think she must be yelling at me, but she's staring right at Mrs. Sweatpants, who is frozen in place, her hands still out in front of her as if she could magically make the shelves reassemble by doing a whammy through the end of her fingertips. "How long do you think it takes us to sort out these shoes? To put them on the rack? To make everything nice?" Liz's round face is bright red, and her perm is bouncing up and down because her whole body is shaking. Then she wags a finger, like she's acting on TV, but it's for real. "Why must you waste my time? Look at you! I have to do this all day! And for what? For you? So you can mess the whole thing up? What about me?"

The woman breaks her freeze and takes a step back because she probably thinks, like I do, that Liz is about to slap her right across the face.

The other customers in the store have turned their attention away from the jumble of shoes and collapsed shelves and now focus on Mrs. Sweatpants. Soon, everyone in the store just stares at her. We're all just waiting for some kind of answer, I suppose, but instead, the woman slowly turns, like she's walking underwater, and glides past the coats and umbrellas and through the front doors, eyes front, chin up in the air, like nothing happened.

I start picking up the shoes, one at a time, then dig through the pile for a partner and line them up on the floor in a pair when I make a match. Liz tries to put the shelves back together. She groans while she struggles with the hardware. When I offer to help, she hisses and bangs the shelves harder.

While she wrestles with the shelves, the guy with the O-rings comes over to ask for some help, and Liz barks at me, "Finish those shoes! Get those shelves back up and do a count while you're at it." Then she pats her hair back down, plasters a fake smile on her face and says, "Certainly, sir," in the not-even-a-little-bit-shrill voice she saves for customers only and follows him to the back of the shop.

I manage to get the shelves back into place, then pair up and reshelve the shoes for the next three hours, while Liz helps the customers who trickle in. We don't get a lot of customers, besides the Christmas rush, when people seem to think a rubber garden hose would make a nice gift for a loved one, but still, it never ceases to amaze me how many people come for door stoppers and inflatable beach balls. Although, mostly they come for the shoes. When you walk around here, you can see maybe half of all the people here creaking around in our ugly shoes – not the rich people, obviously, but they don't live around here.

Apart from the fact that Liz is kind of a bigger bitch than usual and doesn't talk to me, the day goes on like it does any other day: it stinks, it's boring and customers tell me to hurry up at the cash register, as if they didn't just spend twenty minutes trying to decide if they wanted a green hose or a black hose and are now actually in a big rush because they're missing an important meeting. Sometimes I say to Liz, "Late for AA again!" as someone bullets out of the shop, but I'm pretty sure she would find it even less funny today than she usually does. I swear, I would be friends with her if she let me – I mean, I've tried – but she's just sour.

At lunch, I don't even bother sitting in the lunchroom because I need to get out of the stink, and I just know Liz'll cut my break shorter than my usual measly forty minutes and make me do something stupid that she could do herself because she's extra grouchy today.

I take a walk down to the seawall and watch the water. It would be a pretty nice break if I didn't feel so nauseated, even in the fresh air, and though I should probably eat my Marmite sandwich, because I need the calories, the doctor said, I throw it in bits to the seagulls and watch them while they fight and scream. "Just like my folks, aren't ya?" I tell them and laugh, then feel sorry for myself for a while because it's funny, but it's true. "I won't be like that." I put my hand over my stomach. My buttons are going to pop soon. I'll have to get a new uniform.

When I get back, Liz puts on her coat and says for the first time ever, "I'm going out." She turns for one last shot before she steps out the door. "Don't do anything stupid."

As soon as she leaves, I ignore the two customers who are busily messing up the shoes again and go into the office. I lift the handset off the office phone (for the manager only, but she's not here) and call Matt right away, and when he answers after about twenty-seven rings I say, "Hey, baby. She's coming over there. She just left."

Matt swears mid-yawn then howls, "Why?" like he just lost his life savings – not that he has any. He knows she'll be there any second. Liz lives depressingly close to the store.

"Did you tell her?" I ask, as if I didn't know. "Does she know?"

"I didn't give her the deets. Don't you."

"Why not?"

"Shit. Gotta go." Just like that, as if we didn't have a million things to talk about now that everything's changed.

Liz gets back fifteen minutes after her allotted break time is over. I tap my wristwatch and say, "You're in trouble, Mrs. Liz, fifteen minutes," and try to make the expression she makes when I'm sometimes late in the morning after staying up half the night with Matt on the beach with the people he knows – I think they're a bad influence on him, especially now, but he doesn't care what I think. Liz won't meet my eye. Definitely her perm has lost some of its spring.

She could at least tell me off for being smart, but she just goes into the office to put her things away, then reappears with the vacuum cleaner and starts cleaning the rug by the front door, even though it's only two thirty and we're not supposed to do that until ten to five. She drags the vacuum head across the surface, stabbing at the carpet sometimes with the cleaner tube. She pulls and pushes so hard she starts to break a sweat; dark circles appear on the underarms of her uniform, making it uglier, which I didn't think was actually possible.

"Are you okay?" I ask, when she has finished the carpet and comes to stand beside me in the booth where I've been filing my nails, which, unlike her, I'm not allowed to do because the customers can see me and they will think I'm lazy.

The look on her face! Right away, I know she knows.

I give her my best smile, but she turns away.

She could be happy about it, if she wanted to. It's not so bad, is it?

I'm actually relieved when I see Mrs. Sweatpants reappear at the front doors. If it's anything like last time, she'll take ages, and by then we'll be into the late-afternoon rush, and I won't have to talk to Liz for the rest of the day. I expect the woman to go and start pawing over the sneakers again with her chubby hands. Instead, she comes up to the counter.

I'm about to say, "Can I help you?" like I'm supposed to, but she holds her hand up to keep me quiet. Her palm is a very pale pink and pillowy. For a moment, I have the desire to take her hand and hold it. I bet it would be baby soft.

With her other hand, she points at Liz. Then she takes a big breath and starts an actual speech, that sounds prepared and everything, even though her voice shakes. "That was very cruel, what you did to me. Knocking those shoes over was an accident. You should be kinder to the people who come and shop here." She stops and thinks about it a bit, then takes a gulp and starts to improvise. "You should be kinder to people. I'm not working, and my son is very sick." She turns to me then too, her doll-eyes wide. I never yelled at her for knocking down the shelf, but somehow, she wants me to think that her feeling bad is my fault too. Finally, to no one in particular, she says, her pretty voice breaking, "This is the best I can do. I don't have any money. I don't have any shoes."

Then it's the weirdest thing, because Liz comes out from behind the counter, and she walks up to that woman in her falling-down sweatpants and slippers and puts her arms out and hugs her, hard, her cheek on the woman's cheek. "I'm sorry, I'm sorry," Liz says, over and over again, like it was her own fault for knocking down everything, not the woman's, and maybe I imagine it, but I think Liz is crying because afterward she sniffs and blinks when she goes back into the office. She stays in there for the rest of the day without saying one word to me. Between serving customers, I keep glancing at the top of her curly head through the sliding window, but she never looks up.

Even though it gets pretty busy after four o'clock, I look after the customers myself, and you might think I was extra nice to them too, even the elderly man who tries five different raincoats and doesn't buy a single one, but really, I'm only being professional, because I need this job or my dad says I'm out on the street, and obviously I can do it. It's not difficult.

At five o'clock, after all the stragglers have finally left, when I'm getting my bag from under the service desk and Liz is locking the front doors, Matt appears out front, just as she clicks the deadbolt. I haven't seen him for a couple of weeks, and he doesn't look good. He knocks on the doors and his lips make the words, "Mum, let me in." Liz stares at him through the glass but doesn't move. He's become wiry and tense, and he paces in front of the doors, his unlaced basketball shoes slapping on the concrete. He runs his hands through his hair like he wants to pull it out. Liz glances back at me. I'm frozen in place, my handbag held against my stomach like a shield.

He knocks again, heavily, then bangs with his fist. "Mum!" His muffled yelling comes through the glass. "Mum, let me in!"

Liz bows her head and leans against the door, her hands flat against the glass. Matt waits, but when she doesn't look up after a while, he goes crazy outside. He thumps and yells, kicks the doors and they rattle and buckle. A pedestrian approaches, then scurries across the road, so he doesn't have to pass Matt or pay any attention to what's happening.

Liz's forehead bounces against the glass, like she's made out of rubber herself, like she won't break, no matter what. Finally, she raises her head, shakes it, steps back from the door and turns her back to him, until she's facing me.

"You fucking bitch!" Matt screams so loud I bet the whole town can hear him. "It's all your fault." He kicks again, then whines, "Give me some fucking money!"

It's not him. Not really. He can't help it when he gets like this. But still.

He gives up, stops yelling, throws his head back in disgust and stalks away, his hands deep in his pockets, like he's trying to pull himself back together. Through it all, Liz stares at my handbag, concentrating really hard, as if she's making a wish.

"He's gone," I say. She begins to cry. "Liz." I drop my bag, walk over and put my arms around her, all the way. She's smaller than I thought, smaller than me, her shoulders narrow and slight. Her brown uniform hangs off her like a paper bag. I lean my cheek against her head and feel the softness of her curly hair. "Shh," I say, and rock her gently, like she's my child. "It'll be okay," I whisper, over and over. "It'll be okay." But we both know I'm lying.

BREACH

"Wanna make a bet, Mandy?"

Thom stares as the waitress's ass disappears inside, through the patio doors. The waitress has white-girl dreadlocks and a nose ring and a black band T-shirt with an alligator on the front – just Thom's type and nothing like Amanda. Amanda is pretty enough – slender and brown-haired – but ordinary. Boring. After they had been together for a few weeks, she overheard Thom on the phone to someone, saying, "You'd look, but you wouldn't look twice," and Amanda knew he was talking about her, because it was true.

"Yeah, Mands?" Thom laughs and tips his chair back from the table. He would only offer to make a bet if he thought Amanda would lose. "Yeah? See who can get laid first?"

"What?" Amanda turns her head. She must have misheard.

"See who can get laid first, when we're in Quebec."

"I'm going for a piss." Jennie jumps up, pushes her chair back hard. She's Amanda's roommate and had been friends with Thom in university. The three of them are leaving on a road trip in two days.

"I'll win, obviously," Thom gloats. "Let's face it."

"Don't you care if I –"

"Nah!" He turns his attention back to the waitress, who is serving the table next to them. He leers openly, arms folded, feet stretched out in front. "I really don't give a fuck what you do."

Amanda feels a tearing, then, an unmooring of herself and her body. The sensation is familiar and well-practised, though it has not happened since she left New Zealand. She hadn't expected it here, had hoped it wouldn't happen, but a few seconds later, she floats above herself, looks down to where her body sits across the table from Thom, in the middle of a busy patio on Baldwin Street filled with art students, who all sit for hours with a single beer, a Moleskine and a mechanical pencil. Thom is seated near the wall of the café, a converted Victorian house, under the shade of the narrow, blue-striped awning, and Amanda's body, diagonal to him, is drenched in the punishing afternoon sun. She holds one hand over her forehead to block the glare and wraps the other hand around the pint glass she hunches over. Amanda-at-the-table looks small, then smaller, as watching-Amanda, Amanda-in-the-air, floats upward, weightless.

Amanda-at-the-table says, just barely, "Okay?" Then "What do you mean, exactly?"

"What do you mean, exactly?" Thom mimics the tightness of Amanda's voice, her Kiwi accent. "Fifty quid."

Amanda-in-the-air hangs where it's easier to breathe while Amanda sips and swallows her lager, then stares at the fascinating foam on the drink's surface.

Thom has almost-yellow eyes and lank, dark-blond hair, and he is still deeply tanned and ingrained with dirt from hitching out to the Rockies and back. He's lost weight, too, and is nearly slim. Eight weeks with just a bivy bag and the three hundred dollars Amanda lent him and hasn't got back. She had thought his free spirit was romantic. Was that what drew her to him?

"What's going on now?" Jennie thumps her wallet on the table and sits down. She narrows her eyes at Amanda, as though Amanda has encouraged it, this thing Thom does.

"Mandy bet me fifty quid she'll get laid before I do," Thom says. "She's gonna lose though."

"We don't have quid here, tosser," Jennie says. "What did you do that for?" She shakes her head at Amanda, then snorts at Thom.

"Well, whatever; she won't bloody lose. Have you looked at yourself lately?"

Thom grins. "I look hard, me. Sexy beast. That waitress would blow me any time. Right, Mands?" At-the-table-Amanda dips a finger in the foam, then licks it, as if she hasn't heard him. "Yeah, Amanda's gaga for me too. Stupid cow, aren't ya?"

"You don't even have fifty bucks," Jennie says to Thom.

He gently shakes Amanda's shoulder. "Nah. If I lose, I'll have to borrow it off you." He gets up. "I'm not gonna lose though. See ya, love," he says to the waitress on his way out, leaving Amanda with the bill.

"What the hell is wrong with you? Why would you agree to that?"

But Amanda-in-the-air is too far away to answer, floating across the beautiful day, the wide blue sky.

A few months earlier, Amanda had broken up with Sunil. He was twenty-two, a year younger than her, and did something or other in shipping. He lived at home still because he was saving for a house, and he drove a new car. She had met him at Savage Garden late one night when she was staggeringly drunk. He had charmed Amanda by telling her he would never have guessed she was in grad school, though he did acknowledge that getting a PhD in Philosophy wasn't nearly as hard as becoming an actual doctor, and she had agreed.

He seemed impressed, though, by her education, because as he explained once, he thought it proved he was intelligent too, since he was going out with her. Amanda suspected he would ask her to marry him, even though they had only been dating for six months, because he already had plans to introduce her to his extended family and the timing was right according to the life goals he had mapped out for himself on a whiteboard above his single bed. He was the diamond ring type and probably already had one stashed away somewhere. He had told her he loved her and prodded her daily for a reply she couldn't give.

Amanda hated diamonds for a start, but hated even more his cloying niceness. She dumped him over the phone.

Every day for a week after that he showed up at the front door right after work, and at first Amanda refused to see him, but by day six, she felt so guilty as she watched him give up and trail back down the front path to his black, perfectly clean Honda Civic, she had nearly given in and run after him.

"Don't!" Jennie had said from Amanda's bedroom doorway. "He's a knob-end and you don't even like him."

"Okay, you're right."

Assent was easier. Always. But it was hard to know if you were agreeing to the right things. If "yes" would hurt you less, or more.

Thom had arrived in the middle of the night, a couple of days after Sunil was gone for good. His knocking woke Amanda. She went downstairs in her long T-shirt and bare feet and peered at him through the ancient thick glass at the top of the door. He was slightly fuzzy through the window, under the outside light, but she thought he looked familiar. She opened the door.

"I could be a murderer, you know," was the first thing he said. "Nah, I'm Jennie's friend. Just came from England. Long bloody way from the airport too." He had no suitcase, just a Thai bag stuffed with clothing slung across his body and a ratty, handmade sweater tied around his waist. "Let us in then."

"Does she know you're coming? She didn't say anything to me."

"Oi, Jennie!" he'd bellowed up the stairs.

Amanda had led him to the kitchen, where he'd sat down in

one of the mismatched chairs at the long kitchen table, rolled some tobacco into a smoke and lit it. He sucked down the first few drags, one after another.

"You're not allowed to smoke in here." Amanda stood tensely in the doorway and wished Jennie would hurry up.

Thom tapped his smoke over a saucer, then leaned back in the chair, crossed his ankle over his knee. "And what, you're not allowed to sit in here? Or do you just not sit?"

"I'm going to go back to bed, actually. I have an early class tomorrow."

"Do you?" Thom dragged on his cigarette and stared at Amanda through the rising smoke for longer than he should. "Actually?" He imitated her accent.

Amanda sat down.

"There's a good girl." Thom stretched and yawned. "Make us a cuppa though, would ya?"

By the time Jennie got downstairs, Amanda already knew they wouldn't need to blow up the air mattress because Thom would be sleeping with her.

Because Thom can't drive, Jennie and Amanda make a plan to swap driving every three hours from Toronto until they get to Quebec City, their overnight stop on the way to Tadoussac. Jennie had suggested the trip because their classes would be over and she wanted to see the whales in the St. Lawrence, and Amanda wanted to go because she aspired to Jennie's bravery and independence, and she had never seen a whale either. Jennie rented a car, and they agreed to share the cost between the three of them, with Amanda covering Thom's share until he could pay her back after he returned to the UK.

"I don't want him to go home," Amanda says as she loads the car with Jennie while Thom takes a rare shower.

"I can't think why."

"Why what?" But Amanda knows why. "He's not afraid of anything. He just lives –"

"Lives off you, and you don't have any money, remember?"

"My scholarship!"

"Which is how much?"

"Enough. I have money from babysitting too."

Jennie makes her disapproving face. "What, six dollars an hour? He's not –"

"Under the table! And it doesn't matter. He'll pay me back. Anyway, he's *your* friend. You introduced us." Amanda was vaguely nauseated. With Thom back, she hasn't been getting enough sleep. He liked to stay up until three or four in the morning smoking weed and listening to music and wanted her to stay up with him. The sex too. That kept her up. At least her coursework was over.

Thom appears then, unusually clean and clean-clothed for the car ride. "Let the games begin!" He rubs his hands together, then claps, ready to get down to business.

"You mean the stupid bet? Fuck off." Jennie slams the car trunk shut. "See what I mean, Mands?"

Thom gurgles with laughter and lightly punches Amanda on her upper arm.

"We're still doing that?"

"Scared you're gonna lose, aren't ya?"

Amanda has dressed for the trip in a vintage dress she had found in Kensington, her favourite because she thinks it makes her look edgy and interesting.

Thom stands back and examines her. "By the way, what the fuck are you wearing?"

There is the sudden tearing at Amanda's edges, and a few moments later, Amanda-in-the-air yells from the clouds, "The stupid bet, Amanda! The stupid bet!" But Amanda-on-the-ground can't hear what floating-Amanda is saying and wouldn't understand it if she could.

When Amanda is up high, she is out of reach. But it is also disorienting to fall apart. It steals pieces of her memory, and she finds it harder and harder to be happy when she puts herself back together. But she also knows she is safer this way.

They set off, and Amanda sits in the back until they make their first stop at a roadside McDonald's where they buy only fries because Jennie and Thom are vegetarian, and now Amanda is too. And they smoke cigarettes at the picnic table outside because they both smoke, and now Amanda does too. Thom says to Jennie, "I still can't believe you rented a car. Posh now, are we?"

"Go ahead, hitchhike instead." Jennie flicks her butt at his feet.

When they all get back into the car, it's Amanda's turn to drive. Jennie sits in the front seat beside her, and almost immediately, Thom falls asleep in the back and begins to snore.

"Really? He only just woke up."

"We didn't get much sleep last night." Amanda giggles.

"Ew. Shut up."

"Why are you angry with me? Are you jealous?"

"Oh yeah, I'm fucking jealous."

Amanda is pretty sure Jennie is being sarcastic, but she also doesn't want to bet on it that Jennie doesn't mean it for real. Her head feels hot from the effort of trying to make sense of things. "Well, I'm sorry then," Amanda says, even though she doesn't really know why she is apologizing.

"Wake me up when you need a break." Jennie puts her feet up on the dashboard, leans her head against the window and closes her eyes.

It's mostly quiet in the car then, and when her turn is supposed to be over, Amanda keeps driving and lets Jennie sleep on. The Trans-Canada is straight and easy with almost no traffic after

Montreal. Amanda watches the white lines on the road and feels her hands grip ten and two on the steering wheel. It's like she's in one of those dreams where you're stuck on a road you can't get off and you just drive and drive because the road is there, unfolding in front of you, and you follow it and follow it until you are falling from the peak of a bridge that has suddenly disappeared. It's terrifying to keep going. But what choice do you have?

They pitch their tents on the grounds of a dilapidated motel on the outskirts of Quebec City, then walk to a rough, cheap bar, already busy in the early evening, where they begin to drink steadily.

After an hour or so, the bartender wraps his massive paw around Amanda's hand, where he had just deposited her change from the latest round of drinks. He yanks her forward and says, up close, "'Ere, we tip." He must have noted her accent, assumed she was new to the country and had no idea how to behave. He squeezes her hand so heavily that Amanda's nails dig into her palm. "Check ben ça," he says to the other bartender and laughs. Flicks his eyes to Amanda's chest. At last, he lets her hand go, and she drops some loonies on the bar. Deep red half-moons mark her palms. She downs her third pint quickly, quicker than Jennie and Thom even, then buys another and leaves a bigger tip. The bartender, nearly fifty and solid, with a boxer's face, grins at her with all his teeth, like he wants to eat her.

A throng of students, home for the summer or just passing through, surges up to the bar, and Amanda is pushed backward by the crowd and separated from Jennie and Thom. They have been ignoring her anyway, as they drink with concentration and bicker about old times and remember the coolest raves Amanda has never been to and the coolest people Amanda doesn't know. Thom is Jennie's ex-boyfriend's best friend. Jennie tolerates Thom, she told

Amanda, only because she wants to know what her ex is up to now, to connect to him still in some meagre way. He broke her heart.

As more students push forward, Amanda is siphoned to the back of the room, farthest from the bar, against the wall by the window.

"Are you alone?" A man, thirty or so, not much taller than her, but broad and stocky and already thinning on top, leans into her heavily. He buries his nose in her hair. "You smell bien. So good. Aromatique." He is not Québécois. "Tu es très belle, ma cherie."

Amanda tries to duck and release herself from his arm, but the man swings around so he's facing her. He squeezes her shoulder. "Relax." He slides his other hand under her T-shirt, worms his fingers beneath her bra.

Amanda-in-the-air can see how small Amanda looks, how weak, how drunk – just as well. It was better for that Amanda not to know.

"Très belle. Come home with me." He stumbles closer, presses his groin hard against her and tries to plant his open mouth on hers, his tongue already dangling between his moist lips in antici-pation. Amanda leans sideways to escape. Behind the man, Thom pushes his way through the crowd.

"I'm sorry," she says. "I have a boyfriend. He'll be here any second." Amanda-in-the-air watches Amanda's mouth form the words.

The man staggers two steps backward. "Fucking little tease."

A young woman in the group next to them sneers at Amanda, then starts giggling with her friends.

"I'm sorry," Amanda says again, but the man has already dis-appeared into the squirming mass of people. She pulls her T-shirt back down. It's cropped and shows her navel, her bare stomach. Thom liked it. She shouldn't have worn it.

With one hand on her elbow, one on her back, Thom push-pulls

Amanda to the entrance, Jennie following. As soon as Amanda flings her body out the swing doors onto the sidewalk, she is hit by a wall of drunkenness and falls to her knees.

"No wonder he didn't bother," Thom says.

"Shut up, Thom," Jennie says. "For Christ's sake."

"The bet's still on," Thom says to Amanda, where she crouches at his feet. "You couldn't even fucking win it when you had the chance. I'm *golden*. Did you see that blond minge at the bar? Jennie said I had to come and save you though, so you fucked up my chances." He looks at her for a few minutes, sighs and ruffles the top of her head. "Let's go anyway. Full of fucking losers. You can do better than that cock."

It wasn't far back to the motel. As Jennie and Thom, arm in arm, stagger along the narrow and empty back streets, Amanda crawls behind them on her hands and knees, Amanda-in-the-air above her the entire way. At some point, Jennie tries to pull Amanda to her feet, but Amanda refuses. "I like it down here," she says, giggling as though it's a childish game. Both Amanda's palms and both her knees are bleeding by the time they make it to their tent, and there is a deep gash on one of Amanda's knees that looks like it would leave her with a scar for the rest of her life. But Amanda-in-the-air doesn't feel a thing.

Amanda lets Jennie wipe up the blood and cover her with Band-Aids, then Amanda collapses on top of her sleeping bag. "I'm okay," Amanda murmurs. "I learned this trick, a long time ago, so it doesn't hurt."

"What the fuck are you talking about?" Jennie says from far away. Thom falls onto the bedroll beside her. Then Amanda is asleep.

They wake late and have to rip down and stuff the tents into bags and pack them in the car in a hurry. The sun is high in the sky and blazing. Another beautiful day. Somewhere close is the thump of heavy construction deep in the earth, a terrifying booming. Amanda puts her hands over her ears, but she can still feel it in her chest. "Don't make me drive," Amanda begs. "I'm still drunk, I think." Jennie must feel sorry for her because she lets Amanda lie in the back seat for the four-hour drive to the mouth of the Saguenay fjord.

On the short ferry ride that joins the broken highway, a sharp wind blows off the glacial waters, and Amanda begins to feel better. She leans against the railing and scans the water for whales, but nothing breaks the surface. When she begins to shiver, Thom stands behind her and wraps her up in his jacket, crossing his arms in front of her, and she rests her head against his chest. He kisses the top of her head, and she figures it out, at last. The bet was just a joke.

The three agree that Amanda and Thom will pitch the tent while Jennie drives into town to get supplies. The campground is open and grassy, and they are told to set up on a slope that looks down over the bay. They claim a spot beneath two thin trees for the small amount of shade they give. As soon as the tent is up, they crawl inside, undress and fall asleep immediately, naked, entwined.

Amanda wakes after about an hour. It's getting too hot and she's hungry. She hasn't eaten anything all day except for a bag of Cheetos from the gas station in the morning. The memory of the snack makes her immediately thirsty, and she begins to dig in her backpack for some clean clothes. Once she's dressed, she'll try to find Jennie, see if she is back with water and food.

"Hey." Thom watches her, eyes half closed. "Come back to bed."

"I'm thirsty. Too hot." Amanda finds, at last, some clean underwear at the bottom of her pack.

Thom pushes himself to sitting and pulls the underwear out of her hand. "Come back to bed."

"Don't." She tries to snatch the underwear back, but he dangles them out of her reach. "I need some water."

He tugs on her hand, disturbing her balance, and she falls backward. "I don't want you to go," he croons, stroking her hair. "Stay here."

Amanda begins to pull up, but Thom rolls over and drops his leg across Amanda's lower body.

"Stop it," Amanda says, thumping him lightly on the arm, laughing. But there is something else: a tiny bubble of fear deep in her chest. "Get off me."

She pushes him, but he won't take his leg away. Instead, he rolls farther until Amanda is almost entirely beneath him and pinned to the ground.

He snickers as she struggles to get out from under his body; he is much heavier than she is.

"Get off me."

"Haha," he singsongs, but his face is tight. A muscle in his jaw twitches.

"Come on." Amanda can barely breathe. "Please."

He only sniffs in reply, reaches across her, into his backpack. He pulls out a spare guy rope.

"What's that for?" Amanda whispers in a child's voice.

High above the earth, Amanda-in-the-air floats for a while, aimlessly, over the choppy St. Lawrence River. People on the ferry look up at the fine white clouds and taste the icy wind but don't notice her at all. She comes closer and looks down on the small village of Tadoussac. Situated on a perfect crescent bay and overlooked by a pretty, red-roofed hotel, it looks like a magical village in a fairy tale, in which everyone who lives there is really someone or something else and everything precious is dangerous.

When the sun begins to sink, Amanda-in-the-air decides it's probably safe to go back to the tent. By then, Amanda-in-the-tent is drinking whiskey with Thom, gulping it down straight from the bottle and laughing hard.

The next morning, the sky is solid grey, and a freezing wind blows off the water. Jennie leads Amanda and Thom to a booth by the beach where they can buy tickets to take a Zodiac into the bay for whale-watching. "I want to be right there," Jennie says, "close enough to touch them."

"You can't touch them!" Amanda says. "We should just go on one of the ferries. It's cheaper." She hates boats, especially small ones. Hates the way they shift and tip. She's so stupid; of course she has to go on a boat to see whales. She wishes she had never agreed to come.

"Oh, come on!" Jennie says. "You're scared of everything. You don't do anything."

"I do," Amanda says. She looks out over the bay. There are boats everywhere, full of people.

"For fuck's sake, Amanda. If you really don't want to, we can take a ferry."

"No. You're right. The Zodiac looks awesome."

They are given clothes to wear on the boat – yellow rain pants and orange slickers, black weatherproof gloves, black woollen toques – and once they are dressed, they lower themselves from the dock into the low, inflatable boat. It rocks wildly on the unsteady surface of the water, and Amanda shakes in her bones even though they haven't even left the dock. She pretends she's not afraid. Jennie is still annoyed with her, and Thom has moved to the far end of the Zodiac, away from Amanda, where he chats to two young women. There are sixteen people altogether on the boat, and Thom is the loudest, nearly yelling. "Hitching," Amanda hears him say and "next time" and "bloody brilliant" and "chicks." The motor roars and the guide begins to speak through the sound system. Then Thom is only pantomime, mouthing words Amanda can't hear.

They motor out into the bay. Once they are moving, the boat pitches less, and Amanda tries to relax. She focuses on the red-and-white hotel to stop herself from feeling sick and afraid.

Jennie grabs Amanda's arm. "Look!" She points to where a seal lifts its head then dips it again just under the surface of the water.

At the sight, Amanda claps her hands with sudden joy. "Oh my God! I love him!" The girls laugh together at the seal's suspicious expression. Amanda is not scared then, even when the Zodiac continues a little farther out into the sea-like river and the choppiness increases. Soon, whale after whale breaches right beside the boat until the Zodiac is surrounded by their long, knobby spines. In the near distance, feathery plumes rise into the air like smoke. Amanda can hear the hiss of the whales' breath and imagines, fearlessly, the water beneath the boat teeming with the huge animals. A humpback slides through the water beside them before slapping its tail on the surface and diving back into the deep water. Everyone claps. Amanda has never seen anything so beautiful.

The guide cuts the motor and the Zodiac lurches, tipping and bowing on the wavelets; he draws their attention to another cluster of spines in front and to their left, where a pod of whales feed on the rich krill. When Amanda turns to watch them, she sees that Thom has his hand on the back of one of the girls from Quebec. He winks at Amanda when he sees her looking, gives her a thumbs-up with his free hand and mouths "I win." Amanda turns away to face the river on the other side of the boat.

But just before Amanda-in-the-air can separate and rise once more above the bay, the boat tips to the left side and on the right side, in front of Amanda, a humpback leaps out of the water, its face toward the sky, soaring and twisting gracefully in the air, water spraying like light off its back and head. It falls with a slap before disappearing below. Water splashes across the side of the boat where Amanda stands. She gasps and whips her head. It happened so quickly. No one else is looking. She tugs Jennie's coat. "Did you see that?"

"What?" Jennie turns toward Amanda, away from the group of feeding whales.

Amanda points to the water. "You must have felt the splash. Heard it. It was –" Amanda can hardly breathe. She wants to say, "miraculous."

"What?" Jennie says again, sharply, because Amanda is distracting her from the spectacle on the other side of the boat.

"A humpback, jumping! It came right out of the water. Its whole body."

"There wasn't!"

"I saw it. Right there. Right beside me. It sprayed water all over."

"You can't have," Jennie insists. "We would have noticed it."

"I'm sure I saw it." But did she? The image is already fading.

"Jesus, Amanda." Jennie turns back to look with the others. One of the whales in the pod spouts and everyone claps again.

Amanda stares at the blank water where the humpback dived and feels a breach inside her, an empty space where a person used to be. There is nothing in front of her but the choppy surface, whipped up by the freezing wind.

"No!" Amanda touches her cheek, still wet from the whale's splash. "I felt it."

IT MEANS "BELOVED"

"He's a beaut, I reckon," says Brendan. Course he would. "A bargain."

Vic asks him again how much.

"Three fifty. Only, I'll give him to you for three. Mates rates." He puts his hand out, as if the deal's done.

"Three hundred? Nah. What do I want a dog for?"

"Just look at him, Vic." Brendan tugs the dog's collar. The dog jumps down from the back seat and sits on the asphalt. They're out in the Birkenhead RSA car park, next to Brendan's van, which he's parked diagonally over two spaces. Probably pissed before he even got there. The dog puts his nose in the air and sniffs.

"Name's Philip."

"As fucking if. Philip's no name for a dog like that."

Brendan pulls the leash, makes the dog stand, so Vic can see all of him. He's short-haired, brown and white in patches and spots, long-legged and long-bodied. A little stump of a tail. His ears are nice. Silky.

"Call him whatever you want. He's a pure breed, aren't ya?" Brendan slaps his giant palm gently on the dog's back a few times and the dog shivers with pleasure. "He's a pointer."

The dog's ear pours through Vic's hand, then he scratches the dog's neck until the tail gets going. "Where'd you get him?"

"Friend of a friend."

"Just like you; always up to ya elbows in some bloody thing."

"This bloke I know, can't keep him. He was training the dog up, though, for hunting and that. Ducks, I reckon." Brendan takes off his woolly hat and shoves it in the pocket of his shorts, scratches his bald spot, then his nose, lumpy from all the booze. "I can't keep him. Not at my place. You know. Anyway, thought you might be interested."

"Why couldn't the other guy keep him?"

"I dunno. Missus prob'ly."

"Yeah, well, my own missus'd have something to say about it if I showed up with this bloody mutt."

"Wear the pants, bro." He punches Vic lightly at the top of his arm.

The dog's lean, muscular. His spine speed bumps under Vic's hand. "We used to go hunting, eh? All the time."

Brendan's face gets droopy. "Yup. Yup, before –" He stops. He's not a total idiot. He's not gonna just come right out and say it. "Yeah, well, that's why I thought of ya, mate."

The dog dances sideways, then leans against Vic's leg, looks up, like he's figured him all out. "He likes ya! Guess he doesn't know what a cunt you are yet." Brendan pisses himself at his own joke for a while, doubles over and slaps his thigh until he takes a deep breath in. "Nah, really though, Vic." Wipes the tears out of his eyes. "He likes you. I can tell."

Three hundred. Thing is, Brendan has just watched Vic win two hundred and twenty bucks on a trifecta, and Vic's wife, Trisha, is none the wiser. "I'll have to let you know."

"Yup. Yeah, nah, it's okay, mate. Talk to Trisha, maybe? She'll be right, I reckon."

"Hardly. Trisha has precisely zero enthusiasm for anything these days. I know exactly what she'll say."

"Okay. I'll hold on to him, mate. Case you change your mind. Coupla days?" Brendan puts the dog back in the van, cranks the window down a centimetre and they go back into the club and sink a few more pints before Brendan drives Vic home.

· · ·

When Vic shows up at his house with the dog a few days later, Trisha looks at him like he's a lunatic. "*What's* his name?"

"Rasmus."

"What does that mean?" She stops at the bottom of the back stairs, keeping her distance, then takes a draw on her Rothmans. Her lips shrivel and pinch around the filter.

"Heard it on the telly."

"That's a bloody stupid name for a dog." She folds her arms and patters her foot up and down, tap tap, like a schoolteacher. It's past noon, and even though they're standing outside, she wears her dressing gown and the slippers Margie bought from work and gave to her for Mother's Day once, way back. "What do we need a dog for? God's sake, Vic."

"He's not gonna just lie around the house all day and piss on the lawn. He'll be some protection for you."

"From what?"

"Burglars."

"Burglars?" She snorts and blows a big puff of smoke out her nose.

She used to be a beauty. Tall, blond, long legs. No tits, but still – a miracle for a red-haired, wiry bloke like Vic. "She was just in a hurry to get the fuck away from her mother," Vic tells Brendan on more than one occasion. "The smokes have done her in though. Dried her out. And the rest of it."

Trisha looks over the hedge like there's something interesting over there, but there's only a shitty wooden bungalow, identical to theirs except the paint's bright white, not peeling, and the lawn looks like it's been cut with a pair of scissors. "So, how much money did you waste on him?"

"Nothing, I said! Bloke at the RSA gave him to me. He's just a mutt."

Trisha cocks her head to the side and scratches the side of her nose with a long, curved fingernail. "He looks like a pointer."

"What would you know?"

"I know things, Vic. I'm not stupid." She sighs heavily and blows out another lungful. Wrinkles her nose. "Where's he supposed to sleep? Not in the house."

"I'm gonna build him his own house. Right there, by the feijoa tree."

"Yeah? Like the tree house you never finished?" She points at a dying plum tree, battered planks still half-attached.

"I finished it. It's just . . ." Vic slides his hand over Rasmus's satin head, and he turns and licks the tips of his fingers. "What's the fucking point? You can keep your yap shut, can't ya, Rasmus? Not like some people."

Trisha spins and goes back inside. "He's still gonna be pissing all over the lawn, genius." The back door slams shut.

Vic yells after her, anyway. "That's what you're like – pick a fight then walk away." Rasmus leans against his leg, and for a moment Vic doesn't feel like shit for a change. "You and me now, Ras. You and me."

All Vic's junk's still in the garage, right where he left it – the tools and wood, nails and screws. It's damp in there and a mess, thick cobwebs on everything, but it'll all be good as new with a bit of a wipe and a bit of oil, when he gets on it.

Margie used to come and watch Vic in the garage all the time, when he made stuff, when it was his shop. He'd let her use the hammer sometimes, bang a nail in, or turn the Vise-Grip.

"Safety, though!" he had told her. "Never touch my tools unless I say so; no bare feet; that turps'll rot you from the inside out so don't touch it; never, never ever come in here by yourself." And she didn't. She had listened to him when she was small. That didn't last long.

Vic slaps the doghouse together, easy as, then he has the bright idea to cover it with some lino offcuts he got from work as a proper roof. Once the whole thing's outside, he adds a little porch where Rasmus can lie down outside, out of the mud. On the left side of the house, he whacks an iron fence rail deep into the ground and sticks a short chain through a hole in the rail and then attaches the other end to Rasmus's collar. When Vic's finished, Rasmus can run around the yard, but not too far, and he can have a sleep in his house on an old blanket when he gets tired. It's a good house.

"Lie down, boy," Vic tells Rasmus, once everything's set, and he's on the chain. Rasmus tiptoes around, snorts at the grass. The rain drizzles from thin grey clouds, the day clammy as shit.

Trisha comes out to have a look. She's still not dressed, and can't even muster a "well done," just watches while Rasmus shuffles himself round and around into a comfortable position on his new porch.

"I'll take him out next weekend, I reckon. Out to Drury, maybe. Used to go there remember? Roast duck on the table for Sunday dinner again, eh? Like –" Vic nearly says "before" but the word won't come out of his mouth. He means, before Margie grew up. Before she killed herself. Trisha knows what he means. They just stand there and look at each other across the lawn.

"I'm not going to cook the bloody thing. Or clean it."

Typical. She's gonna be stuck in her dressing gown and slippers forever. "Well, I'm off to meet Brendan at the pub."

"Course you are."

Brendan and his mates are good at buying rounds, so when Vic gets home, it's nearly three in the morning and the dog starts kicking up a racket when he staggers up the path. "Rasmus," Vic growls at him. "Quiet! Quiet! Lie down." His chain rattles in his house then stops. Vic crouches down and scratches him behind the ears. Rasmus whimpers softly.

"Ya must have missed me." Vic puts his face against the dog's smooth back. "Sorry, mate. I forgot to feed ya, poor bugger. I'll do a better job. Promise."

Inside the house, it's pitch-black and Vic crashes into all the shit lying around everywhere – Trisha's magazines, the laundry basket and other crap, pot plants. The bedroom door's shut, and Trisha's yelling is coming through it. "The bloody dog howled all bloody day! The neighbours are going to end up calling the cops. You better do something about it!"

"Fuck 'em. You can't just have a tiny bit of compassion for once, instead of complaining all the time."

He chucks some food in a bowl and takes it outside. Rasmus swallows it in about three gulps, then Vic lies down on the damp grass and listens to the dog snoring in his house, curled up on his blanket, and he feels protective, somehow.

The birds' chitchat annoys him at first, but the sun wakes Vic up proper, as soon as it rises above the next-door neighbour's roof. He's soaked, shivering and his head throbs.

Rasmus noses in his empty bowl. When he notices Vic's awake, he slobbers on his face, and Vic has to push him away. Then he gets up to drag himself back inside. Rasmus whimpers a little bit when he sees Vic going, and Vic tells him to shut it.

After Vic's had a shower and chucked his overalls on, he takes out Rasmus's breakfast. "Here." He puts the bowl on the doghouse porch, then puts his hand up, palm flat. "Wait." The dog bounds forward, ready to slurp it all down. "No!" Vic says, harsh and loud, and pulls on the chain. "Wait." One hand still up, he loosens his hold on the chain with the other. The dog rushes forward again. Vic yanks back on the chain and whacks him on the nose. The dog's little tail drops down and his shoulders slouch. "Ya gotta listen to me." Rasmus cocks his head to one side, like he is listening, just like Vic told him. "Go on." Vic lets go of the chain, and Rasmus scarfs his food. He's a good dog.

"No bloody howling," Vic tells him when he leaves later. "Keep your trap shut."

At work, same old, rolling and hauling lino. It breaks his back, and his hands get ripped to shit. Worse though today, even, since he slices his hand open with the lino knife. Half an hour off work – unpaid – to get the stupid thing seen to. Then if it could get any worse, it does, because Hemi calls everyone into the smoko room and tells them they're on overtime now, like it or lump it, seven to seven. Vic needs to unwind after work, so there's no way he can be home before ten.

Rasmus is happy as punch to see Vic when he gets home after midnight. He pats Rasmus on his head. "Good boy, aren't ya, mate? Who's a good boy?" Vic sits with him a bit and wishes he had more time for him. "I want to get out with you, but just can't swing it, not right now 'cause of work. But soon."

Trisha is still up when Vic goes inside. A bloody miracle. "They've got us on overtime now." He collapses in a chair.

She doesn't say a word, just points at the warmer drawer on the bottom of the stove and Vic, drunk and tired, takes the plate out. It's the same thing every night – sausages, mashed potatoes and frozen peas, the whole thing shrivelled to shit. It's an accusation, he reckons, that dried-up dinner every night.

"Not speaking to me then? What did I do now?"

"Get rid of the dog."

Vic takes a long time to finish chewing his mouthful. Trisha watches as his jaws go up and down. "Nup."

"He barked all day."

"He's stopped howling then." Vic points his knife at her. "He's my dog. Mind your own business."

"Bloody typical," she says. "You never listen to me, but I have to deal with it."

Vic knows where she's going to go next. Old story. He keeps shovelling his dinner, chewing, chewing. She should stop, but she won't.

"You didn't listen to me about Margie –"

Vic picks up his plate and throws it at the wall. Peas go flying. "You know what I like most about that dog? He might howl and that, but otherwise, he keeps his mouth shut." He gets up from the table and Trisha backs out of the room.

After she's slammed her bedroom door, Vic hears her slide the dresser in front of it. He yells through the door, "Unconditional. That's what it is with a dog. You're not taking that away from me."

Trisha turns the radio up loud to drown him out.

Trisha doesn't bother Vic for the rest of the week, just stays out of his way, but sometimes when he gets home, there's a rope or a ball on the lawn. She's playing with Rasmus. Just like Vic told her not to. Just to piss him off. They don't listen, women. And Margie – well.

Friday night's a late one. It must be two or three by the time Vic feeds the dog then staggers into the house. The kitchen's a bloody mess, like usual – dirty dishes in a pile beside the sink and ants in a trail from the bottom of the fridge to the toaster. There's a note on the table: *Take him for a bloody walk!* For a minute, Vic's veins get hot, and he wants to smash open her bedroom door and tell her off. Then something wakes Rasmus, and he starts to bark, so Vic has to go and shut him up instead. He picks up a gumboot from the porch to throw at him, but soon as Rasmus sees Vic, the dog stops barking and snorts, happy. Rasmus gets down with his rump in the air like he wants to play, and all the fight goes out of Vic. He gets his jacket and the leash.

It's cold as and there's a massive moon. They walk down the driveway that leads to the park, then up and out of the valley, side by side, their breath blowing in the air like smoke.

There's hardly any traffic this late, just a faint hum somewhere off. No cars go by. Lots of the houses on the hillside still have their lights on though. People sitting up and watching TV. Sitting round the table talking. Vic can't fathom it. Never did that, not even as a kid. He was dragged up. Nine brothers and sisters, and they all looked after themselves. Their mum and dad shit-faced all the time. Used to pack the kids in the car and make them wait half the night while they went to the pub, then drove them home, swerving all over the bloody road. Vic never did that with Margie! But he doesn't know if he can remember what he ever talked about with Margie either. If they ever talked. She hid things from him; that's the truth. She hid everything. Then it was too late.

Maybe if he'd known. If they'd talked. But he'd never asked though, if he was being honest about it.

Rasmus trots ahead, pulls at the lead, then stops, lifts his nose and sniffs at something he knows is there but can't see.

After they get home, Vic settles the dog, washes all the dishes, puts everything away and writes "Happy now?" on Trisha's note.

• • •

As soon as the sun piddles through the venetian blinds, the dog goes mental outside. Then there's someone thumping on the back door, yelling. Brendan. He calls out again. Vic rolls off the sofa, rotten as all fuck, still dressed from the day before and with a massive crick in his neck.

Brendan's wide awake and too bloody chipper. "It's all in my van, guns and that. Camo too. Boots."

Vic stands there like an idiot in his wrinkled coveralls.

"Hunting, bro. Remember? Last night at the pub?" Brendan tugs his hat down farther, till it meets his eyebrows.

"Now?" Beside his doghouse, Rasmus jumps up and down. The collar strains against his throat. "You got him going."

"Yeah, well, he needs to get out, eh? Like you said. Where's the missus? Never see her now."

"No way she's up yet, mate."

Brendan snorts; shows the gap in his top teeth. "Make me an instant, bro, then we'll piss off."

They down a couple of coffees each, then drive across the harbour bridge through mist thick as custard to some inlet off Manukau Harbour Vic's never even heard of.

When they get there, Brendan makes them fuck around in the marsh trying to find a place he says is a good spot. Vic's dizzy as shit from having only three hours' sleep and all the booze on top of that. The boots Brendan's lent him are too big, and his feet keep sliding out, and his socks get wet. The dog runs backward and forward sniffing every hunk of scrub like he doesn't know which way is up. It's a total shit show from the get-go.

"No worries," Brendan says, about a thousand times, while they drag the bag of decoys and all the other crap through piles of mud for ages. The dog just dicks around with not a care in the world and makes Brendan laugh. It annoys the fuck out of Vic when Brendan's like this, but he doesn't have it in him to fight.

Finally, they find the spot and it's good, like Brendan said. The sun's halfway up in the sky now, but soft orange, like an apricot, and not hot enough to burn the mist off the water yet. There are ducks all around, gabbing to each other and dipping their heads in the water. There are tons of other birds, too, right beside them in the bush, calling, or flying overhead.

"This is what it's about, eh?" Brendan slaps Vic on the back.

"Jeez, mate. You look like you're gonna cry."

They set some decoys then get behind the maimai to hide from the ducks. Brendan puffs through his duck caller and calls the ducks back to the water. He looks old. Truth be told, he looks like shit. He's put on the pounds over the years, lost some of his hair. He's permanently red-faced now, and he wheezes when he walks. He's good at calling though – he must have been practising the last few years while Vic was working. Or whatever.

Vic's parched and wishes he had remembered to bring some water.

Soon the ducks are overhead. They skid back onto the pond, and then the hunters scare them up again. There's a massive racket as the ducks explode off the lake and rise into the sky. Vic's too eager and shoots wildly at the shapes above his head. Out of the corner of his eye, Vic can see that Brendan follows carefully with his shotgun – first one duck, bang! Then another. He grins and hoots when the dead ducks fall and splash into the water.

As soon as the birds are down, Brendan unclips the dog's chain, and Rasmus takes off and dives into the pond. He's a champion all right. He comes back quickly, soaking wet and covered in mud, with a mallard in his jaws. Brendan takes the duck easily from the dog and gives Rasmus a scratch. Rasmus wags his whole body and sticks his tongue out like he's smiling. "He's a good dog, eh?" Brendan says, as though Vic doesn't know it himself. "Go on, Ras." Brendan points to where the second duck fell, and Rasmus bounds

119

back out and returns even more pleased with himself. He drops the kill at Brendan's feet.

"Beaut!"

"Dog's freezing now. Dirty as shit too." Vic puts the choke chain over Rasmus's head and starts packing up the shotgun. "He's not a retriever – short hair."

"Nah! She's right, mate! Look at him." Brendan drops his jaw and stares at Vic like he's the one being unreasonable. "Let's go again. You'll get one next time."

"Reckon, do ya?"

"He's thrilled though, bro!"

"Let up. It's too bloody cold."

Vic drags Rasmus back to the van, the choke straining against the dog's throat, then waits for Brendan to get all the decoys and come after him.

Vic doesn't say much on the drive back, but by the time they've had a few at the Razza, he starts to feel better. It's not Brendan's fault Vic's outta practice and bloody useless. "Rasmus did a good job, eh?"

Six pints full, Brendan wraps his arm around Vic's shoulder. "Best dog!" He moves in close enough to Vic like he's gonna kiss him, his head swaying wildly as he tries to keep it upright, and looks up from under his woolly eyebrows. "You'll get one next time we go out, Vic. Yeah, ya will. It's just been a while. You've had hard times. Not a lot of time for hunting."

"You're a good mate, Bren."

Brendan pats Vic's back. "Time for you to move on, Vic."

He's right. Sure he is.

. . .

First thing the next day, Vic decides to take Rasmus out again, just the two of them, to get some shooting in on his own before going out with Brendan again. But when Vic goes outside to feed the dog, Trisha is already out there, dressed even, and some kid is sitting on the lawn, scratching Vic's dog behind the ears.

"Who the hell are you?" The kid buries his face in Rasmus's neck. "Who the hell is that?" Trisha wide-eyes Vic, waves her cigarette and moves toward the house then follows him back inside.

She leans against the kitchen counter, framed by the net curtains on either side of the window above the sink. The sun shines around her head like a halo. It doesn't fool Vic. The curtains are all covered in fly shit.

"Don't upset him!" She talks to him like a child, bossy as. "Try and be nice, Vic, for once."

"Got yourself going by the crack of noon, did ya?"

"That's Darrin, Mimi's kid. She's got a new boyfriend, so I told her he could stay with us for a couple of months."

"Oh my God. A fucking stray?"

"You're one to talk." She takes a deep breath. "I'm going to put him in Margie's room." She stands there with a look on her face like "dare me."

"Nup." It hardly comes out, like he's choking. He takes a step toward her. "No fucking way."

Trisha bends backward from the waist, puts her chin up. "He's only little and there's no one else he can stay with. His grandmother isn't up to it." She can see Vic's face, and even though she knows bloody well what comes next, she doesn't stop talking. "What happens, Vic, when a kid needs help and doesn't get it? If they get turned out when they're in trouble? You should know. You should be pretty, bloody crystal about *that*." She smacks her hand down on the counter beside her, then turns her back, begins to fill the kettle at the sink.

There's a hole behind the back door, where Vic punched it years ago. Frozen, he stares into that hole like it's full of everything he ever lost.

.   .   .

Vic takes the choke chain out into the garden. The kid's still on the lawn with his head down. He's skinny as fuck and wearing a way-too-big Swanndri, pointy knees poking through his ripped jeans. Rasmus leans against him like they're best friends. "You like dogs, eh?"

"Yup," he says, but won't look up, just keeps running his hand down the dog's back.

"Yeah? Well. Not this one." Vic pulls Rasmus away from the kid, then unhooks him from the doghouse and puts his chain on. "Don't come out here and pat him anymore. He's my dog, a working dog. He might look friendly, but he'll bite you if you piss him off."

The kid lifts his head at last and squints at Vic with one good eye. The skin around his other eye is purple-brown, soft and swollen like a rotten apple. His bottom lip is split. "Trisha showed me how to throw him a ball."

"I mean it. Don't fuck around with him! Come on, Ras." They get going, Rasmus yanking on the leash like a bat outta hell, choking and coughing, and they leave the kid by the doghouse, like he could've lived in it himself.

Vic's week goes like this: a long shift, a pint or three, or seven, stagger around the neighbourhood with Rasmus, sleep, then the whole thing all over again. He never sees the kid and pretty much forgets about him. On Thursday night, Brendan and Vic talk about going out again on Saturday. Vic checks the weekend weather on his lunch break. Calculates the best way to set the decoys on a scrap of paper. Imagines how he'll build his own blind.

The phone wakes Vic early as on Saturday. "We've given you a lotta slack, Vic," Boss says. "Sick days, late days. They're piling up. I get it. We're not unsympathetic. But it's been a while. Time to get your shit together. A lotta guys would take your job." Vic has to go in and take a shift and no time and a half because he cut yesterday's order wrong.

Vic wants to tell him to shove it, but says, "Okay, sure thing. Be there soon."

He flings some food to Rasmus on the way past, and Rasmus starts howling before Vic's even at the gate. It's low and loud at first, half-woof, half-yowl, then a long, high-pitched whine that echoes in the valley. "Shut up, ya mutt!" Vic yells across the lawn, but Rasmus keeps at it. Vic can still hear him from inside his van and halfway down the street. "I know exactly how you feel," Vic says. He wants to get out. But no. Stuck a-fucking-gain. "Makes me want to shoot myself in the head."

When he gets home in the afternoon, the kid is sitting on the lawn, throwing a stick a little way for Rasmus, just far enough for the dog to catch it while he's still on his chain. The dog bounds after the stick like a toy poodle, happy as Larry.

"What do you think you're doing?"

Darrin stops throwing the stick. Rasmus crouches, waiting. "He's not mean," the kid mumbles to the ground. "He's lonely, I reckon. He stops howling when I come and play with him."

Rasmus nudges Darrin's leg with his nose, and Darrin reaches out a hand and scratches the dog's chest, then looks up. His eye's not so puffy as it was. Still, he's got other bruises too, like finger-prints, fading yellow, on his wrists, on his neck. "He's never gonna hurt me. Are ya, boy?"

"What's the other guy look like?"

The kid doesn't say anything and chips at the ground with the heel of his sneaker, where Rasmus has already wrecked the grass.

"Fine, you wanna be his friend, you can start looking after him. You feed him every morning, every night. You walk him too. Every day. And make sure the choke's on, or he'll get away." Darrin tries not to smile and hugs Rasmus around the neck. "Don't make him soft though. He's a hunting dog. My dog. Got it?"

Just before Vic makes it inside, Darrin calls out, "Trisha's nice, eh?"

"Suppose so."

And there she is in the kitchen. "Suppose so what?"

"Nothing. You're wearing makeup even? Bloody hell."

She puts her hand up. "I cleaned out Margie's room. All her stuff. Boxed up."

Clear down the hallway, the bedroom door is wide open for the first time since and there's nothing left. All her posters are gone, her knickknacks. Top of her dresser used to be covered with all kinds of shit, perfume and jewellery, bits of paper. Poems, she had told Vic once, but wouldn't let him read them. Not that he ever asked.

"I put the boxes in the garage. Sallies are coming to get the stuff later today."

"Just decided, did you?"

Trisha stares out the window, across the valley.

Vic has to get out of the house then, so he decides to take the dog up to Brendan's even though it's nearly dark and looks like it's going to piss down any minute.

Rasmus trots along beside Vic, relaxed. Waits at the corners when Vic tells him to. He's better behaved with the boy around, but there's no way Vic's going to tell Trisha that.

Brendan can be good for a chat, but when Vic gets there, the bugger's already legless, sprawled on his bed in the shithole garage where he lives, watching racing and downing tinnies faster than anyone'd think was possible. There's nothing on his bed, no blanket, not even sheets. Just a tatty mattress.

He yanks himself upright. "My sister —"

"Trisha's been on the rampage."

"Bitches."

"Believe it, mate. You wouldn't believe what she —"

Brendan blows his nose loudly into a handkerchief, then chucks Vic a DB. Vic cracks it open and joins Brendan in his steady attempt to get as fucked-up as possible. Rasmus dances around all the furniture and boxes of stuff Brendan's sister Carly doesn't want in her house.

"Settle down, ya bloody mutt." Brendan chucks a shoe, and Rasmus sits.

Brendan used to be a bricklayer before the drink got the best of him. He had a life, once. A house. A wife.

"All bitches." He draws the "all" out, like he's moaning.

Vic squeezes himself into a chair in front of the TV, and they watch the racing together.

Brendan's got some bets on and is losing. He swears when the first horse crosses the finish line.

"Trisha's really done it now."

Brendan crushes his empty beer can between his palms and throws it at the wall, then pats the bed for Rasmus to come over. "How are ya, mate?" He holds Rasmus's face and kisses him on the lips.

"Fuck, Brendan! Stop babying him."

"Carly says I gotta go." He motions toward the door with his thumb. "Where the fuck am I gonna —"

"Bloody freezing in here, anyway."

"No one's making ya stay."

After that they just drink silently and watch the horses run around in circles until Brendan passes out.

By the time Vic leaves Brendan's, he can barely put one foot in front of the other. He's lucky he's got Rasmus to drag him home because he's desperate to get there. There's something smouldering in him, in his gut, and it hurts, something he has to tell Trisha. But he can't remember what it is.

At home, when Vic sees the door to Margie's room closed again, the kid sleeping in there, in her bed, the something inside him bursts into white-hot flame.

He kicks at the bottom of the door with his boots to open it, but there's a weight behind it. "Get out of that bed, ya little shit!" He kicks again and when there's a little bit of give he kicks harder. "Get outta there! Out!" He throws his shoulder against the door but can't break it. When at last he stops to get his breath back, Vic can hear the kid in there, sniffling and blubbing. Then Vic's like a bomb going off. He yells and throws his whole body at the door like he's rabid. "Don't cry! Don't *cry*. You're a *boy*. Stop crying. What the fuck is *wrong* with you? Why can't you just get over it?"

"Leave him alone," Trisha says, quiet behind him, trying to calm Vic down. She's got one fist in front of her face, the telephone in her other hand. "Or I'll call the police."

"He's in Margie's room." Jesus. Vic's voice comes out like a fucking squeak, and he nearly falls over, like all his stuffing's gone.

For a moment, Vic imagines she'll stay, put her arms around him and hold him up, but she just calls out, "I'm sorry, Darrin, love, it's okay. Stay in your room; he can't get in. I wouldn't let him anyway. Go back to sleep. I'll be right outside." Her voice shakes.

"I'm not going to hurt you." Vic starts to cry like a little girl.

She stares at him as he slides down the wall into a pathetic heap. "Jesus, Vic."

He wraps his arms around himself and holds his stomach where it burns. "I did it. I kicked her out. And the rest. All my fault."

Trisha nods her head, crying now too. Then she walks away. Closes her bedroom door.

A bang from the kitchen wakes him. He's still on the floor in the hallway. Quiet feet. He pretends to stay asleep but squints his eyes and can see the outline of Darrin in the half-dark, watching. The kid shovels cereal into his mouth, silently, standing up, ready to run. At least he's got survival instincts. Then Rasmus starts barking, and Darrin scoots.

Through the laundry window, in the grey light of the rising sun, Vic can see the kid and dog dancing with each other, Rasmus up on his hind legs, his stumpy tail wagging, front paws on Darrin's shoulders. Then Darrin grabs a rag and dangles it in the dog's face, and Rasmus snaps at it until they're in a tug-of-war, Rasmus growling and shaking his head, and Darrin doing the same thing back. Next, Darrin runs, and Rasmus follows, leaping at him, until they both fall on the ground. The grass is white with frost, but they don't care, just roll around making goofy faces.

Vic grabs Rasmus's chain, chucks on his boots and goes outside.

"Come on," Darrin says, laughing and teasing Rasmus. "Come on, Ras." He pulls back hard on the rag.

"Quit it," Vic tells the kid. "Rasmus!" Darrin drops his end of the rag. They both stop dead and stare. Vic pulls Rasmus by his collar, unhooks him from the doghouse and puts the chain on him. "I'm taking him hunting." Darrin steps back, wraps his skinny arms around his skinnier ribs. "Jeez, I'm not gonna hurt ya." But Darrin steps back again anyway, ducks his head in, terrified. "Look," Vic says, soft for once, "you're an okay kid. Trisha likes you, anyway. I just tied one too many on last night. It's not about you." The kid looks up and nods, then Vic turns down the path, Rasmus trotting beside.

"Can I come?" Darrin says to the gate as it bangs shut.

Vic extracts his twelve-gauge from the safe in the garage, puts it in the back of the van, then goes back and gets all the other shit he'll need for hunting. The wind's coming up, and it's gonna rain for sure, so he stuffs in an extra jacket, waders, a couple of old towels for the dog, some net and poles that he can use to bang together a maimai. Dog goes in the back too. He's still looking right at Vic when Vic slams the door in his face.

When Vic jumps in the van at last, Darrin's in the passenger seat, staring out the windscreen, humming to himself.

"Out!" Darrin puts his fingers in his ears. "Bloody out!"

"I can help you. Carry stuff." He sniffs and wipes his nose with the back of his hand. "I'll do whatever you say. Won't talk too much." He pretends to draw a zip across his lips, then starts talking again straight away. "I've never been hunting before. Bet it's choice, eh?" He pretends to shoot a thrush through the window with an imaginary pistol. "Bam! Bam!" Drops his hands. "I've never done anything before except go to Maccas. We gonna get a Big Mac on the way?"

"Don't touch the gun. Don't mess about at all or you'll have to stay in the van. Stop grinning like a fucking idiot. I mean it."

"Yeah, okay, and then can we go to McDonald's after?"

"Pushing ya luck, aren't ya?"

He starts humming again, so Vic turns up the radio loud and drives.

•　•　•

The city's empty on a Sunday morning. They drive over the harbour bridge and along Highway 1 South, the kid and the dog with their noses against the side window, but there's not much to see on the motorway until they're past the airport. Darrin cranes his neck to get a better look at a couple of low-flying jets. "Cool," he whispers, like he's never seen a goddamn thing in his life.

On the eastern edge of Drury Creek, the air bulges with moisture and the thick smell of mud and sulphur from the overflow. Rasmus gets out of the van, huffs deeply, shakes himself, then bounds away and back, away and back, like he's on a spring. Darrin's found his voice again and eggs Rasmus on.

"He'll scare all the bloody ducks far away before we get out there. He's already good as useless after a week with you." Vic puts Rasmus's neck in the choke and pulls it tight.

"Nah. He's not lonely anymore. He doesn't cry. Trisha told me she's less lonely too."

"Did she just. Well, you'd know about crying, I reckon." That shuts him up.

Vic gets all his gear on and tries to camouflage Darrin best as he can with the spare jacket, then they walk along the creek. Darrin, barefoot, struggles with a bag of decoys but doesn't complain, just grunts now and then with the effort. There are tons of ducks about, flying high above and muttering in the bushes at the edge of the water. When Vic finds a good spot, he begins to put the maimai together and sends Darrin out to find branches to lean against the net.

In a couple of minutes, Darrin comes running back with a handful of leafy sticks and some chunks of gorse. Vic tells him to go and get some more, but immediately the rain starts to come down harder. Rasmus hunches and dips his tail down. Darrin crouches beside him while Vic starts covering the blind. "We need more branches."

"I wish Trisha was my mum. Then I could live with her and Ras forever. Hey, Ras?" Rasmus licks his hand and leans his long damp body against Darrin's leg.

"Yeah, well, she's not and you've already got a mum."

"But my mum's boyfriend hates me. He said so. And Trisha's no one's mum. Not anymore, she said. She said –"

Just then, the rain drops down for real, and they scramble under the blind, useless as it is. But the rain brings a change in the wind that drives the ducks up in the air. Darrin startles and puts his hands over his ears while the birds honk and holler and flap wildly to get themselves airborne before they wheel overhead, scrambling to find new shelter.

"Put these out on the water." Vic pushes the decoy bag over to Darrin. "Down there. We wanna draw the ducks back down in front of us." Darrin puts his arms around Rasmus's neck, but otherwise doesn't move. "Put them out!"

"Rasmus wants to go home."

"Fuck it. I'll do it myself."

Suddenly, with the ducks flown away and the rain nothing more than a soft hiss, it's quiet.

Crouched behind the blind, Darrin strokes Rasmus's head, whispers something in his ear, like Rasmus is his own baby. The dog stretches out his body along the ground and rests his head on his front paws, the two of them taking up all the space.

"Rasmus, come!"

The dog looks at the boy; the boy looks at Vic, hesitates. "Did you ever take Margie hunting with you?"

"For fuck's sake. Take these bloody decoys out there and put them on the water."

"Why are you so mean?"

"Bloody kids, always with the complaints." Vic pulls Darrin out of the blind by his shirt, hard enough that Darrin slips on the slick ground and falls in the mud. When he tries to get up, Vic pushes him back again. And again, laughing like he thinks it's funny.

Finally, Darrin yanks himself up, looks around, trying to figure out which way to run. His face is swollen, holding in the tears he wants to cry. "Go on, ya little shit. Boo hoo. Man up, for fuck's sake." Vic pushes his chest one more time, and Darrin staggers backward but doesn't fall this time. He balls his fists at his sides and leans forward. "Try it." Vic reaches out to take a hold of the kid's scrawny neck, but Rasmus gets in between them, lowers his head and bares his teeth at Vic. "Don't you!" Vic kicks him hard in the rump and Rasmus shrieks and takes off toward the creek, Darrin sprinting after him, slipping and sliding the whole way, getting tangled in the scrub.

"Yeah! Run away!" Vic starts ripping the blind to bits.

The boy and dog stop at the edge of the water. The creek is running high and fast, and there's nowhere for them to go. Darrin turns and stands facing back to where Vic now watches them, Rasmus right beside him, head and tail alert.

The ducks begin to come back. One by one, they swoop in and land behind Darrin and the dog, unafraid, as though the boy called them down himself.

"Rasmus!" Vic wants him back. His dog.

Rasmus doesn't budge.

"You're mean! He hates you. I hate you!"

What's the point?

In the blind, Vic raises his rifle and takes aim. Bang, bang! Rasmus drops. The kid, kneeling over the dog's body, starts screaming blue bloody murder.

When Vic walks down to get him, Darrin comes at him with a stick and Vic throws him sideways. "We're going home."

"Fuck you." He's crying now, sat in a puddle of mud.

Vic grabs his stuff and sets off for the van, but Darrin gets up out of the mud and follows him, tail between his legs, because he's got no other way to get home. Sniffling and moaning. Vic would leave him here, but he'd never hear the end of it from Trisha.

Rasmus is left behind, where he fell. Vic has far too much other shit to carry.

. . .

Darrin keeps up his crying all the way over the harbour bridge, until they're nearly home. He scrunches up against the door, as far away from Vic as possible, one arm across his face, getting snot all over the spare jacket. When Vic tells him to stop blubbing, he just does it harder.

Vic parks at the top of the driveway, but Darrin makes no move to get out of the van.

"Look. Life's not lollies and beer twenty-four hours a day. Shit happens."

The kid growls and bangs on the window with his fist.

"He was vicious. Disloyal. He was fucked-up, mate. There's nothing you can do with a dog like that."

Darrin moves his arm away from his face. The swelling around his eye has nearly gone, but there's still a blackness in there. Deep inside. A hole. It looks right back at Vic.

He wipes his nose with the back of his hand and shakes his head slowly, side to side, before sliding out of the van wordlessly.

"There's nothing you can do," Vic yells after him. "Nothing! Nothing!"

FEELING IN THE FLESH

The gnawing feeling in her abdomen starts a few weeks after Clare finds out she's pregnant, a few days before she takes the two-hour bus ride to see an obstetrician at Auckland Hospital. He tells her that the feeling is probably caused by her morning sickness, and Clare admits that she is retching and spitting thick, acidic gobs of green bile into the kitchen sink every morning after she gets up. The doctor prescribes Diclectin. Clare takes the pills as directed, but the feeling doesn't leave or even diminish; in fact, it becomes more insistent and the vomiting more frequent – at night before bed, in the bathroom at work.

Surely it must be the other way around – it must be the gnawing that causes the sickness – but Clare doesn't bother making an appointment to argue with her obstetrician. He's too busy to talk, and there are no pills for something like that anyway.

Nothing strange shows up on the eight-week ultrasound or the one at twenty weeks, where Clare can see for the first time the baby's fingers, toes and oval-eyed alien face. So only then, once they are home, does Clare mention the gnawing feeling to Simon. "It's a sort of rasping. Like I'm being devoured on the inside." She looks away from him, stares at the shadowy ultrasound image she's stuck to the fridge.

"I can't believe you would say such a thing! You make it sound like the baby's some kind of parasite." He pushes himself up from the small kitchen table with a jerk. In their cramped kitchen, he is suddenly huge.

Clare follows him into the living room. "I don't mean the baby!

No! It's something else." She points to the spot right above the slight rise of her swelling belly. "It feels like it's chewing me here, in the tissue – the fascia." "Fascia." She had looked up the word to make sure.

Simon flops onto the thick, fake-leather sofa, immediately deflated. "It's just nerves, Clare. It was so hard for us to get pregnant." He pulls her down beside him and puts his hand on her, over the baby. "I think you're just anxious that something bad will happen." Worried we might lose it again, he's not saying, like the pregnancy before this one, which was also conceived with a sperm wash in a sterile room at the clinic.

"That's not it," she says. "It's there. There's something . . ."

"It'll be okay." He settles into the dip in the sofa where the springs have failed and flicks on their small TV with the remote. "It'll be okay." He pats her belly lightly with his wide hand, without looking, like she's the baby, not the mother.

Clare tries to distract herself from the feeling with preparations for the baby's arrival. She paints the nursery in a gender-neutral bright green, and when she is at work she shops online and buys wooden toys and cloth diapers when she should be emailing clients. Her decisions are painstaking, and she spends hours searching the Internet and reading reviews and testimonials. She is worried that someone in the IT department will notice her non-work-related computer activity, but still she can't stop surfing, looking for the best things. These decisions keep her up at night: Are plain or coloured blocks better for intellectual stimulation? What kind of natural-wool diaper covers should she order from Australia? How many organic onesies will she need? She also takes up knitting, crocheting and sewing and makes tiny clothes in the evenings and on weekends. Her mother had done the same for her, though Clare cannot do any of these things nearly so well. She often rips back rows of knitting or small, intricate seams to fix her mistakes. "How frustrating," she says to no one in particular, even though what she feels is not frustration but rage at having to do it all over again.

The due date approaches and she practises deep breathing and meditation for her natural birth.

As she surfs the Web, as she knits, below her slow and mindful breathing, the thing chews insistently. Clare pretends it's not there.

The birth is perfect. Clare has trained herself well. On the half-bed in the birthing room, she groans and pants, just the way she is supposed to; she focuses on the baby-animal frieze, which runs around the ceiling, and ignores the cloying lilac walls. Simon tries to help by counting her breaths, but she doesn't need him and waves in his face to push him away.

When the baby's head finally crowns, he stands helplessly and watches, crunching the spicy Doritos he had brought in case the labour was long and he got hungry.

Clare is delirious with the endorphins and can't stop laughing. Everyone had told her that the delivery was the hardest part, but it was so much easier than she thought it would be. She can't believe her luck.

"Hi, Donna," Clare says when the baby has been cleaned and placed on her chest. "Here you are."

Clare and Simon have named the baby after Simon's mother. Clare is estranged from her own; her mother perhaps does not even know Clare was having a baby. "Here you are," she says again. "I missed you."

"Missed her?" Simon asks.

"Oh, you know what I mean."

Donna scans the shadowy contours of Clare's face with calm, grey eyes and doesn't cry.

Clare realizes right then that for the first time in eight months the gnawing feeling is gone.

On the ward, the nurse helps Clare feed the baby, but roughly, pushing Donna's head firmly against Clare's breast. "Won't you damage her neck?" Clare asks, but the nurse just sucks her teeth and ignores the question. The position works well enough. Donna's throat contracts rhythmically, and she half-closes her papery eyelids. It hurts Clare's nipple, but she doesn't want to say so, in case the nurse suggests a bottle. "I have to breastfeed," she told Simon, who admitted that he found the whole thing discomforting. "If you use a bottle, you can break the attachment. I mean, anyone could feed her with a bottle – it wouldn't have to be the mother."

After the feeding, the nurse shows Clare how to swaddle her new baby. Clare is careful to touch Donna as lightly as possible. Her skin is thin and creamy soft; she doesn't have a single blemish.

"Look, you won't break her, darl," the nurse says impatiently. But she could. Donna is delicate, nothing like the fat baby across the aisle, who is slurping a bottle in his young mother's arms. Donna is nothing like that. Clare will have to be careful.

Clare finishes wrapping Donna and slides her onto the thin mattress in the Perspex hospital bassinette. She watches the light fluttering of Donna's eyelashes, the miniscule dip in her nostrils, the rise and fall of her gently sloping chest as she takes each breath. She is perfect.

For the next few days, Clare is happy – no, blissful. She carries Donna from room to room, cradled in her arms, or with the baby's head tucked against her shoulder, and does little else but breastfeed and watch Donna sleep. "You should sleep when the baby sleeps,"

Simon's mother says when she calls from Sydney. "Have you showered?"

"But what if she wakes up when I'm showering?"

"What do you mean?"

"If she wakes up!"

Her mother-in-law is silent for a few seconds.

"Sorry," Clare says before she can respond and more irritated than she should be. "I have to go."

Four days after Donna is born, Clare and Simon take her to the doctor for a checkup. Clare puts Donna in a sling that wraps around her leaky, sagging body. The sling is so deep that Donna curls up and disappears into it, a wonderful secret.

They squeeze their way onto the bus and into the aisle crowded with uniformed teenagers late for school. The teenagers seem enormous. How do children get that big? A tall, animated girl with a pierced eyebrow and a too-short kilt bumps Clare hard by accident and doesn't apologize. Clare nudges Simon, who stares at the girl. "I can't believe Donna will ever be like that. She couldn't be." Clare peeks inside the folded-over sling to get another look at Donna's dainty face and downy eyebrows, which crinkle in her sleep as though she's thinking hard. "I wonder what she's dreaming about."

At the pediatrician's office, the nurse undresses and weighs Donna, and Clare diapers and dresses her again, and then Clare and Simon wait, Clare rigidly upright, on the edge of her seat the whole time in case they are called.

"Should I feed her?" Clare asks.

"She's fine. Maybe I could hold her for a while now. You can read a magazine or something. Stretch your legs."

He reaches tentatively to take the sling, but Clare shakes her head. "I don't want to disturb her."

Finally, the receptionist ushers them into the examination room, where the doctor consults a chart and frowns. "She's a little underweight."

"She's a delicate baby!" Clare says, even though she knows that's not what he means – that "underweight" is not good, no matter what. She bounces Donna in her arms and steps side to side in a slow dance.

"We'll send a lactation consultant to your home to help you with breastfeeding." The doctor doesn't look at Clare, only at the chart on his clipboard, where he scribbles something about Donna's subpar weight.

"When?" Clare asks, but he's already left the room.

"I thought I was doing it right," Clare whispers. "She's happy, isn't she? She's okay?" Simon shrugs. It's a new shrug that started only a couple of days ago – right after Donna was born. It means, "I've never had a baby before. Why ask me?" Clare hates that shrug already, and in an instant, she wonders if she hates Simon and if she has all along.

Their house is a fifteen-minute walk from the bus stop, and Clare is sweaty and tired from the summer heat. Soon the humidity congeals in the air and heavy, warm drops start to fall from the gathering clouds.

"Rain?" Clare looks up. "We have to find some shelter." Her voice is tight and high. "She's going to get wet."

"It's okay," Simon says, striding ahead, not really listening.

"No!" Clare stops in the middle of the sidewalk. "Don't you get it?"

Simon turns and stares at her with his new, confused look. "She's going to get a bit wet. It's fine. It's not cold."

"We have to find some shelter." Clare can barely catch her breath. Her chest tightens, and she begins to pant like a wounded animal. Then, as though someone had just turned a dial and tuned her in, all her senses sharpen, and the world gets bright and clear. She scans the wide, empty street around them, then far into the distance. She lifts her nose, as if she senses some kind of predator. She calculates, then points to the nearest carport. "There!"

"I'm not going to go and sit on someone else's property!" Simon says. "It'll be over any minute, anyway."

The carport is littered with boxes, paint cans and tools, and there is a blemish, an oily patch, the colour of dried blood, on the concrete floor. Clare cowers in the far corner, as far as possible beneath the overhang and away from the rain, her arms around the sling. She shakes so hard, her teeth clack.

Beyond the shelter, thick drops fall but evaporate almost immediately, and just a few minutes later, the sun blazes again. When Clare comes out, still half-crouched, Donna's cries trickle into the steamy air. Simon, barely damp, has not moved.

"What the hell?"

"It might have rained hard. She could have been soaked."

Clare marches home with Simon trailing a few feet behind, and as soon as she is inside, she throws herself on the sofa, undresses and arranges the baby on a pillow for breastfeeding, a complicated process, made even more difficult because Clare is still shaking like something has her in its jaws. She eventually remembers her breathing and draws air deeply and slowly through her nostrils until her milk begins to flow.

Later that night, after Clare and Simon bridge the gap between them with monosyllabic attempts at forgiveness over tinned chicken soup, Simon asks, "What did you think would happen if she got wet?"

"The gnawing thing is back."

Simon shrugs.

For over a year, Donna screams so often and sleeps so little that the days seem to pass by in a painful blur. Clare goes through the motions of motherhood, any thoughts or feelings she has obliterated by the white noise of sleep deprivation. There is an endless pile of cloth diapers to be scrubbed, soaked and hung on the line to dry in the bright, bleaching sun. There is baby food to make from organic kumara, green peas and heirloom pumpkin – food that Donna spits out or refuses altogether. When Simon suggests disposable diapers and food in jars, Clare bristles. "What good am I, if I can't even make her food?" In her exhaustion, Clare registers the grating between her ribs and feels it as little more than a dull discomfort. But on the day Donna wobbles her first few steps across the living room, the white noise snaps off and Clare feels the thing bite down, forcing her to vomit in the kitchen sink. It must have been making a hole inside her all this time. She should have been paying better attention.

That night, Clare keeps a tight hold of Donna and waits at the top of the porch stairs for Simon to come home from work. She can't remember the last time she sat outside. It's too hot in the summer now, and she worries that Donna will get a sunburn or overheat. She hands Donna her sippy cup and says, "Here, drink this," but Donna shakes her head. Clare ignores the gesture, plugs the mouthpiece of the cup into Donna's mouth and tips it back, but the water just dribbles down Donna's chin. Then Clare checks the closure on Donna's hat and yanks it down farther. Donna tugs at it, even though she knows she mustn't, and Clare pulls her hands away, closes them in her own fist to keep them there and says louder than she means to, "Not safe!"

Half an hour later than usual, Simon's figure appears at the end of the street, dragging itself slowly.

"Hi," Simon says dully when he gets to the bottom of the stairs. "What is it now?"

"The thing." Clare lifts a hand to her abdomen. "Remember?"

"I thought that had stopped." Simon sits on the step below them and buries his head in his hands. "Why don't you go to the doctor if you're so worried about it?"

"Do you think I'm sick?"

"Does it matter what I think?" Simon picks up Donna and goes into the house. The screen door bangs behind them.

"It might be a parasite?" Clare says to the doctor.

The doctor raises a perfect eyebrow. "Have you been travelling somewhere tropical? Fiji? Thailand?"

"With a baby?" Clare can't fathom it and nearly laughs. "It's very . . . multicultural here. People come from all over – China, Samoa. Maybe . . ."

The doctor examines Clare's face closely, waiting. "I don't think –"

"Look – there's something there!" Clare points to a spot just beneath her solar plexus. "It's chewing, sort of. Right now. I can feel it." Clare gets up, ready to lie down on the examination table. "Shouldn't you . . . palpate?"

"Do you sleep?" the doctor says without rising from her chair. "How are you getting on with the baby?" She glances at the stroller where Donna takes her single, daily forty-five-minute nap. Usually, she will not nap if she is still, and Clare must walk around and around the block. "She's how old?" The doctor looks at the computer screen on her desk. "About eighteen months, right? So she must be sleeping well by now."

"Of course," Clare lies. She sits back in her chair heavily. "She's always been a very good sleeper."

The doctor is young – younger than Clare; surely too young to be a doctor, or a mother.

The doctor nods as she taps at the computer keyboard. "How

are things with your husband? Are you worried about something?" the doctor asks. "Do you think . . . the feeling you're having . . . could it be anxiety?"

"You sound like my husband." Clare sniggers, as though they're at a bar sharing a joke about the hopelessness of husbands, but inside she burns with rage. "It's not in my head. There's something there. It makes me puke. Every day!"

"But would it hurt to talk to someone? How about –"

"No!" Clare nearly yells. "What if it's cancer and I die?"

The doctor sighs and writes requisitions for an ultrasound and blood tests.

Over the next year and a half there are more tests and specialist appointments: tropical medicine, neurology, oncology. Though he has to arrange for time off work, Simon goes with Clare and holds her hand the first time she gets her test results. It's so long since they touched each other that his hand feels strange to her – thick-skinned, muscular and hairy on the back, like a monster's hand engulfing her own. She shakes loose.

After the third specialist and the second MRI, however, Simon doesn't bother asking Clare about her test results because they are always the same: there's nothing there.

When they are not busing to doctor's appointments, Clare and Donna stay at home and play in the living room or the back garden. They make crafts and read stories and dig in the sandbox. On Tuesdays and Thursdays, they go to Playcentre, where Clare keeps a close watch on Donna and makes sure she doesn't climb the ladder to the slide or play with the child-sized tools. Other mothers watch her sideways and don't talk to her except to ask how old Donna is and what activities she does. Clare tells anyone who asks that they just do activities at home, and after that she keeps to herself. Clare knows that the other mothers are whispering and judging. Sometimes one of the mothers will try to distract Clare or draw Donna away and encourage her to do something dangerous, like use the big shovels in the sandbox, before Clare can put a stop to it. But the other mothers all have easy, well-fed children and big extended families, with grandmothers and grandfathers, and they have no idea what it's like to be on your own.

Most nights, Clare goes to bed early. She lies awake while Donna sleeps beside her on the double bed and feels between her ribs for the rasping thing, but it's slippery under her fingers and always gets away. Sometimes, though, in the half-light, when she sleeps with the blinds open and the moon spills into the room, she can see its shape beneath her pale skin – long and smooth, oval and pointed at the end. "Here it is!" she yells, not minding for once that Donna will awaken. "Quick! Look!"

"Again?" Simon says from the doorway, still in his work clothes. He has staggered from the spare bedroom, where he now sleeps alone every night. "Christ! There's nothing there, Clare!" He doesn't look to where she points.

Sometimes he slams the door, even though it scares Donna, and both she and Clare end up crying for hours.

About a month before Donna's fifth birthday, Simon decides that they should drive to the coast now that they have a car. "Let's at least pretend we're a happy family for once."

"Fine. Let's make a day of it."

Donna will be starting school soon, and Clare has the terrible feeling that she's running out of time. How did they get here so quickly?

By seven o'clock, Simon and Donna have pulled out buckets, spades and sand toys from the sandbox, and together they stuff them into shopping bags in the kitchen.

"A nice drive. The beach . . ." Clare says more to herself than Donna. "I know! I'll make a picnic, with good sandwiches and a cake! Would you like that?"

Donna shrugs as she continues to blow unsuccessfully into a brand new inflatable ring with a tiger's head. Simon takes it off her, and she claps as he blows it up with only ten big puffs.

Clare searches the fridge for sandwich fillings, but they only have peanut butter. She spreads it thickly on not-quite-fresh bread and contemplates making a cake, but the idea overwhelms her. Instead, she stuffs two apples and a half-eaten bag of Tim Tams into the cooler.

"We used to go on picnics, before my father left and –" Clare starts, but Simon is tickling Donna, and Donna is giggling, and neither of them can hear her.

Clare's mother used to fold the tartan blanket and carefully wrap their china in linen napkins. She had woken up early, before anyone else, to make salad rolls with cold ham and lamingtons from scratch. She packed homemade ginger beer. Then they ate all day under the shade of a tree or paddled on the edge of the sea. Until they didn't.

Clare digs frantically in the closet for a blanket and can only find an old sheet. She balls it up and puts it in the cooler with the food and some plastic plates.

She sits suddenly. She rubs the place where the hole is.

"What's wrong, Mama?"

"It hurts."

"Don't!" Simon takes Donna's hand. "I'll get her ready."

.   .   .

On the whole hour and a half drive northwest, Donna sings along to the Wiggles on cassette. Clare sits beside her in the back seat in case Donna gets sick or feels afraid.

"Afraid of what?" Simon asks.

"Don't you understand anything?"

"What is there to be afraid of?" Simon presses.

Clare doesn't know how to answer. There isn't a name for it.

They ascend a slow, sharp mountain, and when they reach the top and begin to descend, they can finally see the beach below. The sea is bigger than Clare remembers and lead-grey because the wind has come up. Clouds draw together on the horizon, then there are distant flashes of lightning and seagulls flutter and fall toward the water before scooping upward at the last minute. A long flat rip pulls out on the southern end.

"The sea!" Donna squeals. "I'm going to be a mermaid."

"Well," Clare says, "I don't think we're going to swim."

"Let her paddle, Clare!" Simon snaps. "For God's sake, let her get her bloody feet wet."

After he parks the car, Simon says, "Can you take some of this stuff and go down with Donna? I'm going to change."

"You're swimming?"

"We're at the beach. What did you think?"

By the time Clare and Donna have scrambled over the tall, powdery dunes, the wind is scattering loose sand in the air and it's much colder. Donna yanks her hand from Clare's and runs toward the water with her pink towel flapping behind her like a cape. When did she get so fast? Her legs are long. She has angles Clare has never seen before.

Clare drops her armful of toys and towels in a heap and runs after Donna, stumbling on the ridges and hollows left by the heavy tide. "Don't go in!"

Donna stops at the edge of the water and watches the dark waves thicken as they surge and swamp each other. She points to two surfers kneeling on their boards in the water, close to the shore, and shrieks, "What is it, Mama?" when Clare catches up.

Clare thinks she can see something too – a shape, just under the surface, flat and pointed on the end – but she can't be sure. Then the fin appears, and the shark pushes its way forward to meet the two boys in wetsuits, who are now only a few metres out. They paddle hard toward the shore with naked hands, and water sprays out behind them. Then, as if in unison, the boys twist their blond heads back to see what's coming. They call out something to one another. The shark is gaining on them fast. The surfers seem to move in slow motion.

"Faster!" Donna squeaks. She pulls away from Clare's grip and steps forward, out of reach.

"We have to go," Clare says, but she can barely make herself heard over the growling waves. "Come!" Clare reaches out to take Donna's arm again, but she's too far away. Clare's feet sink farther into the viscous sand, until she's nearly ankle-deep. She doubles over and wraps her arms around her stomach.

The shark gets closer. With her hands around her mouth, Donna creates a makeshift megaphone and calls out to the boys, "Hurry! Hurry!" Her towel, let go, is stolen by the wind. It crashes and flaps along the sand.

Clare tries to speak, but the words blow out of her mouth. A crushing between her ribs.

A surge in the water lifts the surfboards and thrusts them to the shore, and the boys drag themselves and their boards across the sand before collapsing at Donna's feet. She claps her hands and jumps up and down, triumphant at their escape.

The shark, cresting a few inches now just behind the wave, slows down and circles in the shallows.

"Clare!" Simon has run down to the beach from the top of the dunes. He shakes her shoulder. "What happened?"

Clare doesn't answer and just stares at the boys who lie on their backs on the sand, still at Donna's feet, panting and laughing. Donna is laughing too.

Cold drops begin to fall and lightning flashes again on the horizon. "Let's just go," Simon says. "It was a stupid idea."

"Her towel . . ." Clare gestures vaguely to the tangle that continues its desperate tumble along the beach; it's far away now and obviously lost forever. The sight of it makes Clare's throat catch.

"Forget the towel. It's freezing." Simon lifts Donna into a piggyback before turning and half-jogging back up the beach. He expects Clare to follow and doesn't look back. They disappear past the first line of dunes. The surfers drag their boards up the beach behind them. Low thunder rumbles from somewhere far away.

In the ocean, ten feet or so from the shore, the shark's still there. The fin circles.

Clare tugs her bare feet out of the sand at last and steps into the water. Thick white foam swirls around her ankles. It's freezing cold. At knee-depth, the current tugs her forward, but she stops. Waits. Puts one hand over her eyes like a visor. It's not easy now to find the shark's smooth shape in the turgid water.

There.

The rain spatters.

Waist deep. Clare dips down until the water is up to her chin. It's warmer under the water than exposed to the slicing wind. As soon as she's under, the current pulls her feet up and drags her out quickly. It must be deep. Well above her head. She could sink here, easily, but instead, she kicks her legs hard to stay upright – so she can see it coming.

The horizon disappears. The beach. All that's left is a wall of roaring sea on either side, and now the shark's fin, beside her in the water, the smooth, pointed oval beneath.

147

Clare reaches out her arms. The thing moves in and bites down, making a hole in her chest, just below her solar plexus. What a relief.

KEYS

Amanda sits across from her therapist every Tuesday and Thursday at 2:00 p.m. The therapist looks at Amanda directly and asks questions; Amanda answers them, and her game is not to lie, exactly, but not to tell the truth. She leaves things out. Important things. For instance, she never tells the therapist about the man she is seeing – the men she is seeing – although she knows she probably should. She never mentions the fashion photographer she met online a month after she and Mark had sold the house and moved into separate apartments – how on their first and only date, she had posed for him in his studio loft where he usually took pictures of aspiring lingerie models. He Photoshopped the best picture right there and then. In the edited version, Amanda hardly recognized herself. She looked ten years younger, at least, twenty years younger than him. "See?" he had said. "If you'd put this on your profile, I would have messaged you sooner."

Nor does she tell the therapist about the lawyer, the most recent lawyer, who had showed up two hours later than their arranged meeting time at the Rex. Drunk, his hair a mess, the front of his shirt stained and crookedly buttoned, he laughed contemptuously at Amanda because she had stayed and waited for him, alone, listening to the worst kind of jazz. Less than fifteen minutes after he had arrived, he leaned into her and slurred on sour breath, "You're so tiny, I could pick you up with one hand and throw you." Despite her long and hopeful waiting, Amanda decided this was a good time to leave. The lawyer offered to share a cab, back to his place first? She said yes, then snuck out when he was in the bathroom and jumped on the first streetcar; as far as Amanda was concerned, she had confronted something by leaving, by not just going home with him after all. This was progress. So why bother talking to the therapist about it? There was already enough to talk about.

"What about Mark?" Amanda asks sometimes. "Let's talk about him." But the therapist wants to talk about Amanda, nearly forty and a newly single mother of an eighteen-month-old and a five-year-old. She freelances part-time, haphazardly and for not enough money, finding photographs for textbooks. She can't seem to find equilibrium since her separation, or if she is honest, before that too. She cries a lot and loses her temper, yells at the children and makes them toast for dinner. Because she doesn't know how to make Frank behave or get either child to bed at a reasonable time, they all end up sleeping in her double bed almost every night after falling down, exhausted. Frank kicks and tosses and makes it impossible for Amanda to sleep, and she eventually crawls out from under the covers and lies curled around herself at the foot of the bed, on top of the duvet, like a dog. Most days, she oscillates between rage and misery but is so sleep-deprived she can't tell the difference. Mothering, she has discovered, is much harder than she thought it would be. When the therapist asks Amanda to talk about it, she says, "Why didn't anybody warn me?"

Each week, the therapist asks Amanda to take responsibility for herself, to acknowledge her own part in the making of her messy life: "Who made that decision? Whose fault was that?" the therapist asks when Amanda tells her about her latest failure with the children or her work. She asks gently, then leans back in her chair, fingers laced across her belly and sighs as though she has just enjoyed a good meal. Amanda won't respond; they both know that these aren't really questions, because they both already know the answers.

Sometimes, Amanda says, "I would rather talk about my

dreams. I thought therapy was supposed to be poetic." Then, for a while, they will talk about Amanda's dreams, even though Amanda makes them all up. She can't remember any of her dreams and wouldn't tell the therapist what was in them if she could. The dreams she describes are not lies, though. Amanda makes up her dream stories from her own imagination, after all, from what's inside her own head.

"Last night I dreamed I was driving, but I had no control of the steering," Amanda tells the therapist after a fraught week, the specifics of which Amanda is not willing to discuss. "Then I was on a bridge, but it arched so high in the sky, I couldn't see the other side. I thought the bridge was going to finish in midair, and as soon as I reached the crest, I would plunge into the sea. Then I woke myself up before I fell."

The therapist picks a thread off her pant leg, doesn't make eye contact, tips her head to the side. "What do you think that means?"

"Well, I'm anxious, obviously, and I have no control . . . over my life." It's a good interpretation.

The therapist keeps picking at the thread. "Really?" She looks up at last and smiles brightly, as if Amanda had told her something else entirely. "What will you do this weekend, when the children are with Mark?" Then she waits for a very long time for Amanda to answer.

After nearly five straight minutes, Amanda shrugs and says, "I just remembered another dream, if you want to hear it." She tells the therapist a dream about not remembering her lines for a play. A common dream, apparently; she had read about it online.

Amanda keeps coming to therapy because every time she tells the therapist she's had enough and wants to stop the therapist says, "Clearly you're not ready to stop. It's just avoidance. If you really wanted to stop, you'd just stop. Why do you think we keep talking about it, but nothing changes?"

Amanda theatrically pulls at her hair when the therapist says that, but she never gets up and walks out. Though she's never tried the handle, Amanda is certain the door is locked, and she doesn't want to have to ask the therapist to let her out. She's not entirely sure the therapist will. And what then?

Twice a week for months, the therapist asks about all manner of things that went wrong in Amanda's marriage and all manner of things she is doing wrong now – unable to get the children to bed, unable to say no, unable to find better work, unable to stop spending money she doesn't have on things she doesn't need.

Sometimes Amanda grins and says, "I don't know. It must be my childhood."

Then the therapist slaps the arm of her chair as though she's having a really good time and says earnestly, "Well, tell me about that."

But Amanda doesn't want to tell that story. She doesn't feel connected to her childhood. "I've abandoned that," Amanda says. "It's long gone."

"Abandoned? That's an interesting way to put it, don't you think, considering?"

"It doesn't matter anymore," Amanda insists. She's someone else now. Someone completely different. Not a child.

"I can help you, if you'll let me."

"What do you think I'm doing here?"

"It's not about what I think." The therapist frowns slightly, leans forward. "Why are you here, Amanda?"

"Because Mark cheated on me and destroyed our marriage!"

The therapist swings her head slowly. "That's not it."

Amanda had read Mark's journal while he watched TV with the children on a Saturday morning. She told him that she needed to sleep, but as soon as he shut the bedroom door, she rifled through his backpack for the Moleskine he wrote in every day. Recently he had become even more reserved than usual. It didn't matter if the topic was what to have for dinner or the difficulty she had with Frank at playgroup or her impossible wish they had family nearby to help – when Amanda spoke, Mark focused on a spot on the wall behind Amanda and responded with a low hum. He was already sleeping in the spare room. He couldn't sleep, he said, with Frank in the bed, Lucy waking up three times a night still. He needed his own space.

Then he stayed late at work more often, went away to conferences. There were charges on the Visa bill for restaurants they had not been to together.

She knew it would be there, the evidence in the pages. Mark wouldn't be able to keep himself from writing it all down, so he could read about himself later. But Amanda had been shocked all the same when she found it. There he was, knocking on the woman's hotel room door at a conference, kissing her in the elevator at work. What a cliché.

Amanda launched herself out of bed and down the hallway with the journal in her hand and threw it at Mark. It glanced off his shoulder. He said nothing.

Amanda went into the bathroom, ripped off her clothes and got under the shower, turning the hot tap high enough to be painful and turn her skin red. She screamed under the thump of the water so the kids wouldn't hear her.

When she got out, Frank and Lucy were plonked in front of the TV, and Mark sat calmly on a chair in the corner of their bedroom with his arms folded. "It was only once." Then louder, but measured still, "I can't believe you read my journal. I can't believe you would do that."

"What about 'sorry'? What about 'I love you'?" Amanda wailed, infuriated further by his self-control.

Mark only frowned at her, as if he were the one who got to be angry.

"We have to get therapy then," Amanda said. "You have to come with me, or I'm leaving."

He wouldn't go. And while he wouldn't sleep in the same bed as her or talk to her about their marriage, or anything much at all, he wouldn't leave her either. Amanda had gone to therapy on her own and complained about her impossible situation.

"Then it's up to you," the therapist said in their very first session. "It's your life. You get to decide what happens next." But she doesn't tell Mark they have to separate until she is so thin that her wedding ring falls off her finger on the street and rolls into a drain and she takes it as a sign.

Amanda never tells the therapist that on the weekends, when the kids stay overnight with Mark, she puts on makeup, tight jeans and high heels and goes dancing. She makes herself into the kind of woman she wanted to be when she was younger. Like Margie. Thin, sharp. The kind of woman that men like. Though it didn't help Margie, Amanda wears this person like a costume, or maybe armour.

Still, if she peers closely into the bathroom mirror, Amanda can spot the subtle droop of her eyelids, the tiny fissures running upward from her top lip. There are stretch marks on her breasts and hidden beneath the fly of her low-rise jeans, all over her stomach – tears on the surface of her skin, as though the course of her life is ripping her to pieces in ultra-slow motion. The children had grown there. Now her skin folds and sags between her hips. At night, she lies flat on her back in bed and runs her hand over the dip between her protruding hip bones and wonders where it all went.

•   •   •

At El Convento Rico, Amanda drinks five shots of tequila then dances by herself, bumping up against anyone close as though they are dancing together.

From the edge of the dance floor, a man follows her with his gaze as she spins across the room. Whenever she looks up, she catches him watching her, and when the club closes, he's waiting for her outside. He is younger than her and good-looking. Confident. He leans against a lamppost, a brown European cigarette in the corner of his mouth. As she walks past him, he catches her elbow to steer her the way he wants her to go and says close to her ear, "I like you. Come and have coffee with me."

They sit in Coffee Time under bright fluorescents and drink burnt coffee out of Styrofoam cups. Casually, the man tells her he is rich and asks her to come home with him, so she can see the restaurant he owns.

Amanda holds her scalding coffee and sips it gingerly, tries to decide what to do. Under the bright lights, it's easy to see the loosening of the skin on the backs of her hands.

Frank and Lucy would be fast asleep at Mark's, adorably curled up together because, although Mark won't let the children spend the night in his bed, they can't bear to sleep alone. At least three times, Lucy will get up and cry at Mark's door, and he will tell her to go back to bed, go back to sleep. Frank won't wake up, not even a little bit. Maybe Lucy is up now, crying. "She mostly asks for you," Mark tells her. "'Where's Mama?' Forgets, I guess."

"I can't," Amanda says at last to the young man.

"Why not?"

"I mean, no. I don't want to." She has practised saying "no" with the therapist, but as soon as she says it, she's worried about what comes next.

The man lifts his arms and looks down at his young body and expensive clothes in mock surprise. "You've got to be kidding."

"I just want to sleep."

"Sleep?" he says, his languor gone. He stands up and points a finger in her face. "A whore like you?"

Amanda stares unwaveringly at the tabletop as he leaves, pretends he was never there in the first place.

She stays and finishes her coffee alone. It tastes like cigarette ash, but she gulps it down, burning her tongue and throat, bringing tears to her eyes.

"Hey!" The only other customer, an old man at a table in the back, curls around his coffee cup and donut, protecting them from some imaginary onslaught. Beside him, a wire cart spills plastic shopping bags and odds and ends. "I told you so." He cackles gleefully and tears at his donut. "Told you."

By the time Amanda gets up and walks shakily outside, the streets are nearly empty. A few lost souls drag their belongings and the odd taxi prowls. Amanda decides to splurge and flags one down. She is deeply tired and can barely sit upright in her seat, and when the driver breaks too hard at the lights she lurches forward and has to hold the seat in front to steady herself.

"Don't get sick in my cab." The driver tuts and shakes his head. "At your age."

As soon as she gets home, she goes to bed in her clothes with all the lights on but doesn't fall asleep until sunrise.

Six months after Amanda's separation, the therapist asks, "How much are you drinking?" because Amanda has let it slip that she doesn't feel so great, and that she drank a little bit more than she should have the day before.

"Am I drinking?" she repeats. The question has caught her off guard. She has said too much. "Not much. Not compared to some people I know."

"Which people?" the therapist asks casually. She raises her eyebrows.

Amanda looks out the few inches of window between the not-quite-pulled curtains and glimpses the laneway. It's piled with the garbage containers of all the residents who live in the apartments above the therapist's office. Broken furniture, bikes. A stained mattress is propped against the wall.

"Why won't you look at me?"

Amanda gazes around the room, her eyes resting for a moment on the bookcase directly behind the therapist, then the flowered wallpaper. A brass lamp. A small table with a glass of water. The door is old, solid oak. Before their session begins, the therapist closes it behind her and stands against it for a few minutes while Amanda settles herself. The door has a Victorian glass handle and a keyhole that sometimes has a key in it. Not today. The therapist keeps one hand in her pocket – perhaps the key is in her hand.

"How much is not much?" the therapist presses, but softly, as though the answer doesn't really matter.

Amanda is used to these traps. If Amanda tells her the truth, then the therapist will know it's too much. But if Amanda says, "I don't want to tell you how much," then the therapist will know it's too much. So Amanda outright lies for once and tries to give a reasonable amount, an amount the therapist will believe. "Two. Not every day. Every couple? Sometimes one, sometimes three." It doesn't sound quite right. Is three drinks every couple of days a lot? "More on the weekend, I suppose. Only if Mark has the kids. When I go out. I don't drink when the kids are home."

"You go out." The therapist nods her head slowly, as if she is beginning to understand, at last. "What do you do when you go out?"

Amanda concentrates on a small tear in a tiny rose on the wallpaper. "I have girlfriends! We have dinner, Saturday night, or – but never Sunday. That's when the kids come home from Mark's."

"Three drinks a day?" The therapist sighs, smiles.

"You think I'm an alcoholic."

"Are you?"

"No," Amanda says. "I'm no worse than anybody else I know. There's nothing wrong with me. I don't even know what I'm doing here."

"Then why don't you just leave right now?"

"I am very afraid of making people angry, and you've made it clear that if I leave you will be very, very angry."

"Have I?" the therapist says. "I think you're projecting. Anyway, what could be the harm in going to a meeting?"

On Wednesday nights, Mark comes over to Amanda's apartment, a broken-down, two-bedroom on the ground floor of a Victorian house – the only thing she could afford in the neighbourhood after they sold their home. Amanda goes out to give Mark some more time with Lucy and Frank. They have decided the children are too young to go back and forth during the week. Mark has decided it; Amanda has agreed. He bikes over straight after work and rings their doorbell at five thirty.

Mark doesn't bother with hello, barely looks at Amanda as he hangs his helmet and jacket.

Lucy watches from the living room doorway. Her eyes trail Amanda as she puts on her cardigan and zips up her bag. "When will you be home, Mama?"

"You'll be in bed."

"I've got to get up at six, remember." Mark taps Lucy lightly on the head, but she ducks and shrugs him off. "I mean it. Don't be late again."

"You have no idea what it's like. I'm on my own."

"Whose fault is that?"

"What! You're the one who had the affair!"

"Don't!" Lucy wails. "Don't." She puts her hands over her ears and crouches low.

"Just go." Mark holds the door open.

On the way out, Amanda slips on the top step and her feet come out from underneath her. She catches herself just in time by grabbing the banister but bashes her knee.

She is still shaking by the time she reaches the end of her block, and once she's at the corner, Amanda realizes she doesn't know where to go. Usually, she would have a date, or would have arranged to meet some friends for drinks, but she has resolved not to drink this week. She doesn't have to drink, but she doesn't know how to do dating without drinking, and her friends are busy, and they are drinking friends anyway, so what else would they do?

She tries to ignore the deep throbbing in her knee and walks purposefully along College Street, toward Kensington Market. Although it's mid-week and early and getting colder, the patios are full and no one is alone except her. She thinks that in the market there might be music, or someone reading poetry, but as soon as she's there she's not sure she can sit in a bar and not drink, so she wanders up and down Augusta and looks in the closed store windows. All the market's brightness has been put away. It's just dirty and grey now, with piles of garbage on the curb. It makes Amanda disproportionately sad. This is a particular problem of hers, her therapist has told her more than once, the *disproportionate* nature of her feelings. She has suggested to Amanda that it might be an illness, something chemical, but Amanda won't have that conversation and changes the subject when the therapist brings it up.

Amanda stares for a long time through the fish shop window at two large rats who swirl around each other in the otherwise empty display case. She is not sure if she is filled with horror or anger or something else altogether.

There's nothing to do but walk back home then. She buys a slice of pizza on the way and sits outside the library on a bench but can't bring herself to eat it because she keeps thinking about the rats.

She's home by eight and Mark is pleased. The children too. They go to bed in their own beds for once, and Lucy wraps her arms around Amanda's neck and kisses her sweetly on the cheek before turning over and closing her eyes.

As soon as the children are asleep, Amanda opens the bottle of wine she bought on the way home and drinks it all before falling into bed.

The next week, Amanda goes to AA. She tells the therapist it will give her something to do when Mark has the children.

The nearest meeting on Wednesday nights is in a church basement, just around the corner from her apartment. By the time Amanda gets there, there are already fifteen or twenty people milling around outside. A few denim tuxedos, but also khakis and one knee-length pencil skirt with expensive pumps. It was probably a bad idea to come to a meeting so close to home, but apparently no one else is that reckless because Amanda doesn't recognize anyone as one of her neighbours.

A woman must have singled her out because she comes up to Amanda straight away. She is quite a bit older than Amanda, maybe sixty, but she looks good for her age. Her hair is a well-executed golden blond, and her skin glows beneath thick but perfectly applied makeup. Lipliner, even. She extends her hand, palm down, as if to be kissed. Amanda takes it and the woman squeezes. "Welcome. I'm Barbara. I'm an alcoholic."

Amanda doesn't trust people who say "welcome" and she thinks she will laugh out loud because it's just like she found herself in the middle of a TV cop drama and because she is nervous.

"There are all kinds of people who come here." Barbara takes Amanda's elbow and directs her down the stairs and through the doors. "People just like you." Amanda turns her head to take in the crowd, probably nearly thirty people, who circle one another and get ready for the meeting. It's like a terrible party, where Amanda doesn't know anyone, except worse, because there's nothing to drink.

She lets Barbara introduce her to a thin trickle of shuffling ghosts who stuff themselves with broken Voortman's windmill cookies and swig Coke out of two-litre bottles. "This is Amanda," Barbara says. "She's new to us."

The ghosts say welcome too, and worse, "Congratulations," as if Amanda just won a prize.

When it's time to start, about half the group settle on seats in the main hall, and the other half, Amanda and Barbara among them, file into a small backroom and squish so closely together on chairs that they nearly touch the people on either side at the ankles and knees: Amanda, Barbara and thirteen men, none of them older than thirty, all of them on court-ordered rehab. There is no one just like Amanda.

In the corner of the room, there's a sink and a white boiler to boil the water for huge teapots of tea and above it one grey, grimy window where dirty feet walk by, their owners oblivious to the people beneath them. A small blade fan propped up on the counter moves the stale air around. When she shifts in her seat, the broken edge of the wooden chair catches Amanda's thigh, embedding a splinter above the back of her bruised knee. When it's her turn to introduce herself, Amanda passes. Barbara glares at her.

"So?" the therapist asks at their next session. "How was the meeting?"

"It's exactly like you would imagine it would be, if you weren't under the mistaken notion it would be better."

"It's really something to be so smart, isn't it?" Amanda knows she's not projecting now; the therapist is angry. "We won't get any-where if you're not honest with me."

Amanda sighs and decides to say nothing for the rest of the ses-sion, and they sit silently for an hour while Amanda stares out the window at the cluttered laneway. Finally, the therapist opens the door. She pats Amanda gently on the shoulder on the way out. "It's hard some days. This is what we're here for. See you on Thursday."

Amanda has been chatting online for two weeks with Alex. He brags about being an architect and that he can afford the best drugs, ordered through the dark web and shipped by FedEx from Vancouver. When she meets him at last, Amanda isn't surprised that she doesn't like him at all. He's at least fifteen years older than he said he was, he's not her type and they have nothing in com-mon. Still, ten minutes after she arrives, they smoke hash from hot knives while leaning on the granite kitchen countertops in his Rosedale home, and then it doesn't really matter if she likes him or not. Amanda has sex with him because she has found that it's expected and she doesn't want to disappoint anyone. Luckily, she is high enough to be able to pretend it isn't even happening.

At midnight, Alex tells her that she has to go, his teenage chil-dren are coming early in the morning. She gets dressed quickly, with her back to him, leaving her four-inch heels off to walk down the driveway in the dark to the taxi. She is still unsteady and dis-oriented from the drugs, or something else, she can't tell. As she gets into the back seat, Alex presses three fifty-dollar bills into her hand for the thirty-dollar cab ride.

Amanda cries all the way home and all day on Sunday until Mark drops the kids off. After that she makes soup and toast, and Lucy and Frank eat it kneeling by the coffee table while they watch videos before bed. Amanda has half a bottle of wine and eats nothing but the crusts she's cut from the edges of the toast. She's not hungry, and anyway, there's nothing else because she's behind on her groceries.

When the children are asleep, she prods at the sharp angles of her collarbone, runs her palms down her protruding ribs. Her unfamiliar thinness makes her disproportionately happy and miserable at once.

"What did you do on the weekend?"

"Why do you always ask me what I do? I thought we were supposed to be talking about how I feel?"

"How are you feeling?"

"For fuck's sake! I went out."

"Where did you go?"

"To a friend's house."

"Oh. That's nice. Whose house?"

"Someone I met."

"Where did you meet him?"

"Why do you assume it's a him?"

"I'm sorry. What's her name? How did you meet her?"

"I met him online."

"This could take a while, don't you think?"

Amanda puts her fingers in her ears. "Can we just change the subject now?"

"Do you manipulate men too?" The therapist snickers when Amanda rolls her eyes like an irritated teenager.

Amanda goes to AA again. When it's her turn to speak, she says, "Hi, my name is Amanda, and I'm an alcoholic," just to try it out. Everyone groans, "Hi, Amanda," just like they do on TV, except that in real life the people in the room sound even less interested. After that, she has nothing else to say. She listens as a man with inch-thick glasses tells them that he cries every day but hasn't had a drink in twenty-three years. Amanda thinks a beer would cheer him up. Feet at the window kick up dry dust.

After the meeting, Barbara gives Amanda her phone number and tells her to call if she ever needs to. "You need a sponsor. I only saw you once last week!" Barbara digs one of her perfectly manicured nails into Amanda's arm. "I'll see you tomorrow."

"I've got my kids. I can't come tomorrow."

"Kids? What's more important? You should be here every. Single. Day." She gives Amanda a copy of the Big Book and assures her that though there is a lot of talk in it about God, it's not actually about God.

"I don't believe in God."

"You have to realize you have no real control, and you have to give up trying to control your life. You need to leave it to a higher power."

Amanda thought she was here because she was out of control already. "Higher power sounds a lot like God."

Barbara frowns and leans in close. "I think I know your problem. The trouble with you is that you are arrogant."

"Something has happened!" Amanda has run from the car to the office foyer. She's out of shape and has to catch her breath.

"What is it?" The therapist speaks slowly and tries to mask her alarm. Amanda wonders what she thinks it could be.

"It's just, when I parked, I locked my keys in my car. Stupid, I'm so stupid."

"Okay," the therapist says. "Okay." She gestures to Amanda to enter the room.

"No! We can't just – I don't know what to do now. I have to pick up the kids after this. This has never happened to me before. How am I going to get home?"

The therapist walks into her office, and Amanda follows as if she's drawn by an invisible thread. She paces by the window. The therapist closes the door and waits. When the therapist finally sits, she tells Amanda to sit too, as though she is about to begin, but Amanda paces still. The therapist says calmly, "Now, tell me, why did you lock your keys in your car?"

"What?" Amanda stares at the garbage in the laneway. There is so much of it. It's piled up. Spilling everywhere. She can smell it rotting. The smell coats her mouth. "Where does it all come from?"

"Amanda, sit down."

Amanda stops pacing but won't sit.

"Listen to me," the therapist tries again patiently. "Why did you lock your keys in the car?"

"Really? Really?" Amanda says. "I don't know how to get my keys. I don't know who to call. I can't think straight! I want it to stop. I need my keys! Why won't you just *help* me?"

The therapist answers her as though she is talking to a small child. "I could, if you could understand why you locked them in there in the first place. Why don't you sit down?"

"I don't –" Amanda yells. "I don't understand why you can't just help me!" The room shrinks around her, and she thinks she won't be able to take another breath.

The therapist leans forward, shoves her fist into the pocket of her skirt.

Amanda falls into the chair. She stares at the door handle, then turns to the therapist. "I want to go home."

The therapist nods. "Okay. So, let's begin."

WILL YOU BE A CHRISTIAN?

Amanda dragged herself up the steep zigzag path that led through the bush to Ernie's house with Lucy clinging to her hand. She couldn't have slept more than a couple of hours on the flight from Toronto, and Lucy was overtired from the flight, too, and nervous at seeing her grandfather for the first time. But Frank, only just turned three, ignored Amanda's commands to slow down and ran ahead. Amanda's sister, Judy, trailed a few feet behind.

"God. He never stops, this kid."

"Like Dad," Judy said.

"Fuck that!"

"Hey, the kids!"

"You don't think they're used to it?" Amanda rubbed her bare arms. It was colder in Wellington than she had been expecting. She had forgotten about the dampness. "Jesus. What the hell was Dad thinking when he bought this place?" She concentrated on navigating the path. It was uneven and slick with moisture and decaying leaves. "He's always been so bloody impulsive."

Lucy stumbled and Amanda pulled her right. Lucy was nearly seven, but shy and quiet. She didn't complain when Amanda yanked her up, but continued gingerly, one foot carefully in front of the other, eyes to the ground.

"Don't you want to ask me how Dad is before you see him?" Judy said.

They had talked about the weather and Judy's kids and Amanda's job on the drive from the airport, anything but the reason for Amanda's return home. But now they were here.

"You told me on the phone. I'll see myself anyway, right?"

Judy stopped walking and held Amanda back. "That was a week ago. You should prepare yourself."

"Sure."

Ernie had a glioblastoma, already too far gone for surgery when they found it. He could only wait now as it rapidly took up residence in his brain.

Frank disappeared around the last corner.

"He's going to get there first," Lucy squeaked.

"It's okay. He'll be banging on the door with those chubby little fists. 'Let me in!'" Amanda laughed. His banging would piss Bridie off. Amanda liked the idea of that. Yet, dutifully, she let go of Lucy to catch him before he caused a ruckus. Straight away, the ground was hurtling toward her, and Amanda had to lean against the spongy trunk of a punga tree to steady herself. She closed her eyes for balance and the smell of the bush detritus wadded in her nose. Her mouth filled with the taste of dirt.

"Mama!" Lucy came and wrapped her arms around Amanda's waist.

"Don't worry, Luce. Mama has jet lag." Judy gently pried Lucy away. "Makes you feel a bit crappy when you're a grown-up. Sorry, sis." She rubbed Amanda's back until Amanda could push herself off the tree and continue up the path, Judy hand in hand with Lucy behind her.

By the time they made it to the garden, the back door was already open, and Bridie stood in the doorway shaking Frank's hand – or perhaps grabbing his wrist.

"Don't!" Frank shouted, red-faced.

"He was pulling out my hyssop!" Bridie said.

"Hyssot." Frank nodded his head in agreement.

"I could see him through the window." She wagged a finger at her step-grandson. "Naughty boy."

Amanda scooped Frank up and deposited him on her hip.

"You can't let him run around," Bridie continued. "We're not set up for children. He'll be too much for your father." She turned and went back into the house, but left the door open for them to follow.

"Fucking what?" Amanda hissed.

"She's his wife, Amanda," Judy said, in a voice that unkindly imitated their stepmother's. Judy had a deep dislike of Bridie; it was the only acid in her temperament.

"Your father's asleep," Bridie said as soon as they were in the house. "I need a lie-down myself. It's been a terrible strain." She wiped under her eyes with shaking hands and smiled weakly at Amanda. "Hello, dear. Hello, Lucy." Lucy immediately buried her face in her mother's hip.

Bridie exited, gripping the furniture for support as she went.

"She's strong as a horse," Judy whispered furiously as soon as Bridie had left the room. "And I hate to tell you this, but she's made him change the will. Dad told us the money from the house would come to us, but she brought a lawyer to the hospital."

"Get down!" Frank yelled, pretending to scold himself.

"Shush, Frankie. Quiet." Amanda retrieved him from the chair he was climbing. "Whatever. I don't care."

"Get down!"

"Stop it, Frank!" Lucy put her hands over her ears. "Mama, Grandma will be angry."

"Here. Can you take him?" Amanda held Frank out to Judy. "I really need a cup of tea."

Amanda had only come all the way here, anxious child and terrible toddler dragged along with her, for one thing. She wanted Ernie to own up to his catastrophic failure as a father before he died. She wanted him to say, "It was not your fault. It was all mine." She just wanted him to acknowledge what happened. She didn't care a bit about the will. Money wouldn't make her feel better.

While Judy took Frank and tucked him up with Lucy on the sofa in the living room for a nap, Amanda filled the kettle and put it on the stove to boil. She examined the house, heavily draped and carpeted in varieties of beige and pink, and full of things she had never seen in her life. It was a family home in which she had never existed – Bridie's family, plus Ernie's things. There were tall shelves filled with hardcover bestsellers in multiple editions, and along the plate rails that circled the dining room and living room, hideous china Toby mugs with hooked noses, bulging eyes and oddly shaped hats, like an array of tiny gargoyles, but facing into the house. Knickknacks everywhere. China figurines and lacquered boxes and candelabra – maybe Bridie's, but Ernie had always been a collector. He had collected newspapers and magazines when Amanda and Judy were kids. He kept them in case he needed them, he had said, but never explained what he needed them for, and as soon as a magazine or carefully clipped article was added to a stack, he never looked at it again. Bridie must have trained him out of it, or at least redirected him to more respectable hoarding that included some long-term value, because there were no magazines besides the latest *New Zealand Woman's Weekly* on the dining table.

"Our inheritance," Judy said, gesturing to the things in the room. "What's left of it. Worth what, do you think?"

"Those books aren't worth anything," Amanda said.

"I'd like to keep something though." Judy ran her hands over the spines. "It would remind me of him. You can have those." She pointed to the evil-faced mugs. "If Bridie lets you."

"I don't know that I want to be reminded."

Amanda stepped up to the bay window and looked across the valley to the thick, dark-green bush dotted with pastel-painted Victorian bungalows. The houses seemed to be balanced precipitously on the sharp angles of the earth as it jagged its way down to the inevitable coastline. Amanda would live here, if she could, even with the wind and the punishing inclines. It was a bittersweet landscape, the best kind. Beautiful and unforgiving.

"Oh my God!" Bridie yelped from the kitchen. She must have crept in behind them and now stood, kettle held high in one hand, thick grey smoke pouring from its rubber bottom and the top of the stove. The smoke expanded and billowed into the living area. An acrid scent burned in Amanda's nose. "Oh my God!" Bridie shrieked again. "You're going to set the house on fire! Look at all this smoke!"

Bridie's exclamations woke Lucy and Frank, and Frank immediately began his own wailing in earnest. Amanda ran to the kitchen where she stood helplessly as Bridie ran the kettle under the tap, though she could do nothing about the rubber still melting and smoking on the slow-cooling electric element.

"It's a new kettle! Why did you put it on the stove? It's not that kind!"

"I'm sorry," Amanda said. "I didn't –"

"What's happened?" Ernie staggered into the dining room waving a walking stick in the air, then crashed into the table. He steadied himself against a chair, then fluttered one hand in front of his face to clear the smoke. He was shockingly frail and dishevelled. Amanda had not seen him in over ten years, but still, she had never once before seen her father without a clean shave and a close, careful haircut. It was as if a new face had been exposed, or an old one, one that had been there all along but she hadn't seen, thin-skinned and vulnerable.

"Oh my God, Ern! Look what she did!"

"It's poisonous. Don't breathe it in!" Ernie croaked. "Open the windows!" He tried to make his way forward, but his walking stick clattered to the ground. With one hand, he held onto the chair again, and with the other he pulled a handkerchief out of his pocket and pressed it up to his nose and mouth.

Bridie flung open the back door, then pushed frantically on the window above the sink, then banged at the frame until it finally swung open. "Now it's freezing," she screeched. "We'll catch our death!"

Ernie lifted the handkerchief and waved it around his face. "Get the smoke out. Get it out. It's going to give us all cancer."

Amanda began to cry loudly, in an explosion of tears, like a child. Immediately the room silenced, apart from her sobs. The air seemed immediately clear, the smoke whisked away by the cold outside. Both Frank and Lucy appeared in the kitchen. Frank's jaw hung open, his face still wet from his earlier crying, but no more sound came from him. He galloped over to his mother and wrapped his arms around her knees. Lucy tiptoed up to Judy and stood very still a few inches away from her as though her stillness could make her invisible.

Bridie was suddenly no-nonsense. She patted Amanda on her upper arm and said in her regular voice, "It doesn't matter." She flapped a tea towel in the now-clear air a few times then moved to Ernie. She took his hand. "Sit down, Ern, there you go."

"I'll boil some water in a pot," Judy said.

Amanda wiped her face and calmed herself with a few deep, shaky breaths. "Hi, Dad."

"Ern," Bridie said in an exaggerated tone. "Amanda's here. She's come all the way from Canada with Frank and Lucy."

"Who?"

Bridie pulled out a chair at the table. "Come and sit here with him, Amanda."

Amanda lifted Frank and they sat opposite Ernie at the table, Frank on his mother's knee, uncharacteristically subdued. Lucy sat on the chair beside them, tracing the patterns on the tablecloth with her narrow finger. Ernie's eyes were wide open, as though he were still angry and terrified and disbelieving. Then his face suddenly relaxed and he smiled beatifically. "I've been going to church." He tapped his forehead, between his eyebrows. "God is in here." He seemed to have forgotten about the poisonous smoke already. "God." He bared the soft-pink gums between his few remaining teeth.

"Okay." Ernie had only ever spoken vaguely about God and had never gone to church as far as she knew. In memory of her mother, he had told Amanda they were Presbyterians too, though they weren't. He told her when she was very small that her mother had gone to heaven when she died, but even then, Amanda knew he didn't believe it; he just didn't want to talk to her about what had really happened.

"He's a light," Ernie said. "A white light. Pure brightness! Here." He rapped on his forehead again. "Do you know about Him?"

Lucy stopped tracing. She watched her grandfather carefully.

"That's enough, Ernie," Bridie said. "You'll tire yourself out with all that talk."

Judy brought cups of tea and a plate of biscuits to the table. Frank grabbed for the biscuits and shoved one in his mouth.

"Can I have one please, Mama?" Lucy waited for Amanda to pass the plate.

"How lovely," Bridie said and smiled at Lucy's manners. She held Ernie's hand steady as he lifted his cup to his mouth.

"Dad used to be a missionary," Judy said to Amanda. "Did you know that? When he lived in Sydney. Methodist, weren't you, Dad? When he was about twenty, he handed out pamphlets on street corners. 'Come to the Lord!' And all that. Didn't you, Dad?"

"What are you talking about?" Amanda said. She had never heard anything of the kind.

"Ancient history," Bridie said, and helped Ernie to lift his cup again.

When the cup was safely back in its saucer, Ernie nodded by swaying his upper body backward and forward, though it was not clear he was answering Judy. His eyes travelled along the plate rail. The Toby mugs looked back at him.

"How do you know that?" She couldn't recall even thinking once about her father as a young man because he had never mentioned being young or described what his life was like before he moved to New Zealand and married their mother. They didn't have any family stories. There were no photos from his childhood. Amanda had met her own grandmother only twice, once when she was very young and then again at her grandfather's funeral, but she hadn't really understood that her grandmother was Ernie's mother, and that once he had been a child. She had always imagined him as motherless, like her, but also perpetually her father, as though he had arrived in life a grown-up, fully formed, for that reason.

"Dad's been telling me all kinds of stuff about back then. About Mum. He goes to the Anglican Church now though, don't you, Dad?"

"Your mother. Ah." Ernie closed his eyes.

Amanda waited, searched Judy's face for answers. Judy shrugged.

"Who's this fella?" Ernie opened his eyes again and waggled his eyebrows at Frank. "He's a cute little fella." Ernie turned to Amanda and stared fiercely, as though he were waiting for an answer to an urgent question.

"Your grandson, Frank," Amanda said. "Say 'hello' to Grandpa, Frank." Frank shook his head and leaned into Amanda, hiding his face.

"I was a naughty boy too. That's why they sent me there."

"What do you mean, Dad?" Amanda said.

"And the little girl is Lucy," Bridie said. "What a lovely child."

"Lucy," Ernie repeated.

"Your granddaughter," Bridie said.

"What did you mean, Dad? Sent you where?"

"Who is it?" Ernie said.

"Lucy, your granddaughter! Amanda's daughter!" Bridie yelled as though he were deaf. Lucy looked like she was about to cry; she didn't like loud noises, didn't like being noticed and talked about.

"Have another biscuit, Dad." Judy pushed the plate toward him. Ernie took a biscuit, dipped it in his tea and sucked off the soft end.

"Food means everything to him now." Bridie smiled at her husband benignly. "It's really the only thing he has left."

"Dad, what –"

"And you." Ernie patted Bridie's hand and his eyes filled with tears.

"Oh, such a good man." Bridie teared up too.

Amanda considered hurling her cup of tea at the plate rail, imagined all those ugly little faces smashed to pieces and falling on them like rain.

As soon as the tea was finished, Ernie had to rest again, so Judy drove Amanda, Lucy and Frank to their cheap motel downtown. The kids fell asleep in the back almost immediately.

Amanda had barely had the chance to speak to Ernie because Bridie had held forth the entire time, explaining everything that had happened since Ernie had fallen: his cancer diagnosis, his stay in hospital, his return home, the generous visits from her own children and grandchildren, who loved him as though he were their very own, she said. Ernie had not been able to last long, in any case, and Bridie, though she complained that it would be useless for her to try to sleep again, went to bed with him because she wanted to lie beside him and watch him while he slept.

"She's faking it," Judy insisted as she nervously directed the car down the steep and narrow, twisted streets. "It's all about the house. He doesn't even know which way is up. They've fought like cats and dogs for years. Just like with Helen. Well, maybe not so bad as that – no hot irons being thrown at anyone!" She glanced at Amanda and chuckled, but Amanda didn't find it funny. "You know what I mean. He's not exactly easy to live with, but Bridie? Bloody hell. How could anyone stand it?"

Amanda shrugged and closed her eyes. Although she couldn't exactly fathom Bridie's devotion, she wasn't convinced that Judy was right. She thought Bridie did love him, and stranger, she suspected that he loved Bridie back. It made her feel worse, though, to think so. She had always believed he was incapable of love. Now, it seemed that he was capable, and had simply withheld it from her.

Judy dropped them off and told Amanda she would pick her and the kids up the next afternoon because a nurse was coming in the morning, and Ernie was usually better later in the day, as well. "He's more physically able in the afternoon because the tumours aren't messing with the bits of his brain that make him move. And he has these moments when everything is clear," she said, "when his memory sort of comes into focus, and he tells all these stories about his past."

"Great. So when his memory miraculously comes into focus, does he remember what he did to us?"

"Mands, what's the point?"

"I'm just so fucking angry."

"No kidding."

Amanda would have stormed away then, but Judy took hold of her and hugged her tight. "See you tomorrow."

The kids skipped ahead, even Lucy excited to see the motel room.

• • •

The next morning, jet lag woke Frank around four and he wriggled around in the queen-sized bed they were all sharing, singing to himself. Amanda pretended she was still asleep until five, when Lucy woke too. Then Amanda made them Marmite on toast and tried to sleep a little longer while the kids ate their breakfast and watched TV beside her. When the sun finally came up, they all got dressed and walked down to the beach to look for shells.

It was cold on the sand, but they took their shoes off anyway, to feel the sand beneath their feet. Frank zoomed down to the water's edge where he paddled in the thin sweep made by the low waves. Lucy wouldn't go near the water. She stayed on the beach-side of Amanda, as though her mother's body would protect her from the big sea. Frank ran back and forth, giving Amanda handful after handful of broken and weed-covered shells. Lucy searched carefully for shells that were undamaged and shiny and presented them to Amanda one by one.

Amanda didn't understand why one of her children was so brave and wild, the other so fearful and gentle. Was it her fault that Lucy was anxious? Her fault that Frank was naughty?

The sky was overcast, and soon there was a light spit of rain. The wind came up off the water and pushed at them hard until Lucy was so afraid of the waves, they had to take shelter under a stretch of trees on the grassy area above the sand.

"I don't like it here," Lucy said.

"Sometimes, I feel afraid too," Amanda said, more to herself. "I have something to say to Grandpa, and I don't know how to say it. Now we're here, I don't even know if I should."

"What?" Frank poked at the ground with a piece of driftwood.

"Don't, Mama." Lucy put her head on Amanda's lap.

"I just want him to admit it."

"Don't, Mama!"

"What did you say?" Frank squeaked in his silly voice. "What did you say?" He jumped up and ran down to the water and began throwing rocks at the sea.

Lucy closed her eyes and put her fingers in her ears.

"I wish that worked for me," Amanda said.

"I bought a kettle," Judy said when she arrived that afternoon.

"So did I." Amanda held up a plastic shopping bag. She had taken the children to Farmers and bought the most expensive kettle she could find. The store had the same overstuffed racks of dresses, the same officious service as when Amanda and Judy were kids, shopping on their own for school clothes, a blank cheque from Ernie in Judy's jeans pocket.

"What kind of kettle is it, exactly?" Judy asked. The question put them both into hysterics, and then Amanda felt better about the whole thing.

"Remember how Dad used to always complain about the smoke at work? How all those guys thought he was such a dork because he told them not to smoke inside?" Judy said.

Amanda nodded. He had always been a health nut, even before it became popular. He had become a vegetarian when Amanda was a teenager, took up jogging. "Remember? 'Wash your hands or you'll get hepatitis!' God, he said that all the time!" Amanda laughed.

"*Sunlight* soap only. 'None of that perfumed stuff!'"

"All those showers he took too. Three times a day. What was up with that?"

"He was right about the smoke though," Judy said. "That's probably the reason for the cancer. All that smoke he inhaled. And Mum. She wouldn't have had a heart attack if she hadn't smoked. What are the chances?"

In her head, Amanda said, "No, Judy, you know what gave him cancer? Guilt." She couldn't make the words come out of her mouth, but still, they sounded good to her, like something someone would say in a movie. But did he even feel guilty? "Maybe," she said out loud. "Or nothing. Bad luck. Cancer doesn't give a fuck."

"Fuck!" Frank repeated from the back seat.

"See?" Judy said. "Don't say that, Frankie. It's not nice." She sighed. "It must have been terrible for Dad when Mum died. So stressful to be on his own with us. I don't think we could really understand what it was like for him."

"Him? Oh, that's why he married Helen in such a hurry? So she could look after his 'stress' but beat the shit out of us?"

"Shit shit shit shit shit shit," sang Frank.

"Mama," Lucy said. "Frank is saying bad words. Make him stop."

"Now look what you've done," Judy said. "They pay attention to what you're doing and saying, you know. They copy everything."

When they arrived, Ernie was pacing in the living room with long, eager strides, like a caged tiger, his unsteadiness from the day before gone. It was a dramatic change, as though the cancer had haughtily decided that today he could move and speak. He had paced like this his whole life, in every space, no matter how hospitable, as if he were desperate to escape wherever he was; desperate to escape himself.

Banging and slamming came from another part of the house. Bridie must have been busy somewhere.

As soon as he saw Amanda, Ernie stopped pacing and said, "I have to tell you something!"

Judy took his arm. "Don't you need to sit down, Dad?"

"No," he said. "No! You sit down." He pointed to Amanda. "Sit

179

down there, on the sofa. I have to tell you something."

"Mama, Mama," Frank whined. "Book." He clambered over her to one of the bookcases and began to yank one of Ernie's precious first editions off the shelf. "Mama, story!"

"Who is that? He's wrecking my books."

"It's Frank, Dad." Amanda grabbed Frank by the top of his pants and lifted him across to the other side of her lap. He began to climb over her again, fighting against the firm arms she was now using to restrain him. "Remember, you met him yesterday. He's my son. Your grandson."

"Is it Judy?"

"I'm Judy. I'm grown up now. This is Amanda. She's come all the way from Canada to see you. These are her children, Frank and Lucy."

"I know who Amanda is!"

"Book!" Frank yelled. "Mama!"

Ernie stared at Lucy, half-hidden behind the sofa. "Canada? What were you doing in Canada, Amanda?"

"*I'm* Amanda. I left, Dad. Remember? A long time ago. I went to university there." Frank dug his tiny, sharp-nailed fingers into her arm. It hurt. "Stop it!"

"No!" Frank flicked his head back and smacked his hard skull against her jaw.

"Jesus!" Tears welled in Amanda's eyes. She rubbed the spot where his head had made contact. "That bloody hurt. Stop it!"

"Amanda," Ernie said. "You look just like your mother. I met your mother when I went away to New Zealand. I left my family too. She was so beautiful. We went dancing. She hugged me. Such precious kisses. Then you, Judy." He shook his head. "We had to get married. But I wanted to."

"What about Mum?" Amanda said as she struggled to squeeze Frank into a spot beside her where he couldn't move. "Did she want to get married?"

"It's okay, Dad," Judy said. "We know she did."

"When she died . . ." Ernie stared at Amanda. "I didn't know what to do."

"Mama." Frank pushed his feet as hard as he could against Amanda's thigh.

"Frank! That hurts!"

"You've got to believe me," Ernie said, ignoring Amanda's struggle with her toddler. "I hadn't . . . Oh, my father. When I was a boy, they sent me away. Then, Helen."

"You married Helen." Amanda jumped on the opening. "That's what you did later. Remember? You didn't look after us properly, left us by ourselves all the time. Then you married Helen. She abused us, and you never –"

"I didn't know what to do," he said again, but in a child's voice, and Frank, surprised by the sound, settled for a minute and stared at his grandfather.

"Tell me what happened then, Dad, with Helen." Amanda looked away from Ernie's ragged face.

"Stop it, Amanda," Judy said.

"Stot it!" Frank yelled ferociously and put his hand over his mother's mouth. "Stot!"

"Christ! He's driving me fucking crazy!" Amanda roughly lifted Frank and thrust him toward Judy. "I have no idea how to deal with this kid. Can you take him so I can have five goddamn minutes to talk? He never shuts up." Judy took Frank wordlessly, and he immediately wriggled and kicked out of her arms before running through the kitchen and out into the garden with Judy following.

Lucy, left behind, began to sniffle.

"Go outside too," Amanda snapped. "You don't need to cry. You cry about bloody everything."

"Helen was hard to be married to," Ernie said, pacing again. "It was so hard on me. She –"

181

"Hard on *you*? You were married to Helen for nearly six years. Six! I know you know what happened. Tell me what she did to us, how you ignored it. You knew. You never even tried to stop it."

Ernie stared at the Toby mug faces, as though he were waiting for them to tell him something. Then he shook his head fast. "Wait, wait, wait, wait, Amanda. I have to ask you something. Are you listening? Are you? Are you?"

"What?"

He stopped in front of her, prepared himself, then spoke. "Will you be a Christian?"

Amanda snorted, then laughed out loud. "Did you listen to anything I just said?"

"Will you be a Christian? Will you, for me?"

He would never be sorry. This was how it had always been with him, with them. How naive to expect things to be any different.

"I can't just do that, Dad. You can't just decide to become a Christian for someone else, because someone asks you to. You have to believe it."

"You can believe it! Can't you at least try?"

"No!"

Ernie appeared immediately deflated, all his nervous energy dissipated. His frail body sank in on itself, and he could no longer stand steadily on his own. "I need to lie down now."

He looked up at the plate rail again and spoke to one of the ceramic creatures. "It burns here." He rubbed his forehead hard. Then he turned to Amanda. "Maybe you could pray with someone you know?"

"What good would that do?"

"Come on, Ern, my love." Bridie had bustled into the room. "You've tired him out. Let's get you to bed."

Amanda went outside where Lucy and Frank were digging in the herb garden. Upon seeing her children, all her anger emptied out. She picked up Frank and snuggled him to her. "I'm so sorry, Frankie," she said.

He kissed her on the cheek and handed her a long green stem. Its camphor-like scent reminded Amanda of when she was a child and Ernie, sick with a cold, bent over a steaming bowl of water and eucalyptus, his eyes streaming with tears.

"That's hyssop," Lucy said. "Granny showed us."

"He asked me to be a Christian," Amanda told Judy later, on the ride home, laughing as though she thought it was funny. "Me! He obviously doesn't know the first thing about me."

"How could he? You haven't lived here for fifteen years and have only been back once. You don't call him." She glanced sideways at Amanda, who was now stony-faced. "What did you say when he asked you?"

"What the hell do you think?"

"You could have lied," Judy said quietly.

"I just couldn't," Amanda said. But now she had the terrible feeling she had misunderstood his question and had missed something important. That she had made a terrible mistake and would never be able to fix it.

Ernie deteriorated rapidly and didn't get out of bed again. Amanda visited every day with the children for an hour or so and told him about her life in Canada as though he were an elderly stranger she had come to keep company with chitchat. She helped Bridie as much as she could, and she and Judy took Frank and Lucy to the movies and the museum, walked along the beach, visited the bird sanctuary.

. . .

The day before she was to return home, Amanda found Ernie wide awake in bed. "You look better today." Amanda sat beside him. The skin on his face was nearly transparent now, as if he were lit from within.

"Was it my fault?"

"What are you talking about, Dad?"

"Your divorce, was it my fault?"

"No! Why would you even think such a thing? It has nothing to do with anything. It was just a mistake."

"A bad thing happens and then it never stops."

"What?"

"I couldn't help it."

"Help what?"

"They made me, at that place. But was it my fault? I don't know."

"What bad thing, Dad? Do you mean what happened to us? To me and Judy?"

Ernie's mouth moved desperately, but there was no sound.

"Judy!"

The room was suddenly full. Judy and Bridie bustling around the bed, the children there too and getting in the way.

"Oh no!" Bridie keep repeating. "Oh no."

Amanda was pushed into a chair by a wave of lingering jet lag. She put her head between her knees and tried not to pass out.

A week after Amanda had returned to Toronto, Judy called to tell her that Ernie had died.

"He left her the house, nothing for us."

"Do you need the money?"

"It's not about the money. What of Dad will be left to us? On top of that, Bridie wants to bury him in his slippers. Jesus! He would hate to be buried in slippers."

"I'm sorry I can't be there. Not that it makes any difference now."

"Yeah, better you saw him alive," Judy said. She hesitated. "Did you talk much to him?"

"Not really. He made it pretty clear he didn't want to talk to me about Helen."

"Oh, I mean – he talked a lot to me about himself, about when he was a kid. I wondered if he'd told you –"

"When he was a kid? He did?"

"He told me he had been sent away when he was little, that they sent him to the Sallies. For a bit. A few months."

"The Salvation Army? I don't –"

"Yeah. You know, a home for kids." Judy waited again, but Amanda couldn't speak. Something was coming into focus, and she didn't want to see it. "And I just found out there's a class-action suit in Sydney now because of what happened there. Abuse. You know. Sexual abuse."

He had yelled in his sleep every night, fighting horrors in his dreams. Three showers a day. Nothing feminine, ever.

"He was five."

"Five?" Amanda stared through her window out into the street as if she had never seen the world before. "Fuck."

"He said his mum couldn't cope because he was like Frank." Judy laughed. "Hyper! He liked Frank."

"Why didn't he tell me? I was right there."

"He was scared when he died," Judy said. "The minister from his church came but Dad just kept saying over and over again, 'I'm not forgiven. I'm not forgiven.' I don't know what that was about. He was baptized and all that. Just the cancer, I suppose. He couldn't really make sense of anything by then."

Amanda knew what he meant. But he had it around the wrong way. It wasn't him.

. . .

A few months later a large box arrived at Amanda's apartment by courier from Wellington. Amanda ripped off the tape and Frank clambered over her to see. There was a note on the top from Bridie: "Your father wanted you to have these. I sent Judy the books."

A mob of ugly faces stared up at her from the packing.

"Look," she said to Frank. "Here. Lucy, look. Our inheritance." She handed each of the children a Toby mug and took one for herself. "Let's have a tea party."

"We might break them," Lucy said. "Frankie is clumsy."

"It doesn't matter." Amanda pulled some more mugs out of the box and arranged them in a line on the floor. They were distorted and grotesque, but they didn't look evil anymore, and Amanda noticed for the first time they were all laughing. "It doesn't matter if they break. It's just stuff. We don't have to hold on to things forever."

PURIFY

In the sky, there is no distinction of east and west; people create distinctions out of their own minds and then believe them to be true. – Gautama Buddha

When had it happened? There had been no burst of light. No inexplicable fainting or miraculous speaking in tongues. Goodness, no. No epiphany. It was more like sinking into a warm bath – a slow dissolving, rather than a sudden baptism. Dinah couldn't pinpoint when exactly she considered herself submerged, but it had undeniably happened. She had been in the supermarket checkout line when she had had the feeling, or the idea – the certainty, in fact – that God was there, all around her, soft against the edges of her body. Or maybe there were no edges anymore. She couldn't tell.

For the rest of her seventy-one years, she had been a resolute atheist. "I would like to believe in God," she had explained on more than one occasion, when it was necessary. "It must be comforting. But I don't. I just don't." She had said the same to her neighbour only a couple of months earlier, when Amanda had asked if Dinah would like to join her church choir.

"Who said you had to believe in God?" Amanda snorted in reply, as though it was the most idiotic thing she had ever heard. "You can still come and sing with us. I only go because I like the music."

Amanda was a writing professor at Mohawk College who lived happily with her grown-up daughter in the house next door. When Dinah had moved from Toronto to Hamilton, Amanda became her only acquaintance. Dinah had tried hard to keep to herself, nodding politely and never stopping to chat, but she was finally unable to escape Amanda's attention.

"She is overly generous. Garrulous," she complained to her son, Michael, on the phone after Amanda had delivered a Tupperware box full of homemade muffins. "Enough for ten people. Is she trying to make me fat? She's up and down the street all day, knocking on doors. A do-gooder. You know the type."

"Garrulous? Now, Mother." Michael called her from Calgary weekly, but he was not the slightest bit interested in anything she said.

After Dinah's husband, Alan, had died suddenly right on Bloor Street from a massive heart attack, Michael had convinced Dinah to sell their large Toronto house and move somewhere more manageable. The house, which Alan had bought when he was made partner, was now worth millions, it turned out. Michael was hoping for an inheritance, no doubt, but Alan had put nothing aside for their retirement and had accrued a lot more debt through various disastrous gambles on the stock market than he had seen fit to mention to Dinah. Once the house was sold, there was very little left and Hamilton – an old steel town and much cheaper than Toronto – was her only option. Even still, Michael blamed her, not Alan.

"You are selfishly oblivious to everything," Michael had said when he found out.

"I don't care about money. Your father always took care of that – I thought."

"What did you take care of?"

"You hardly need the money, Michael. What about me?"

When Amanda brought up the choir for a second time, it struck Dinah that perhaps it would be nice to have some social contact. She and Alan had been emotionally distant from one another, but they had been married for a long time, and there was a space in her life where he used to be. A hole. Dinah had hoped that moving away from their home and making a new life for herself would fill it – it did not. So she let Amanda convince her to join the choir, though she pretended she was reluctant and only doing it as a favour.

The choir met every Wednesday in the chapel attached to the sanctuary. It was a small group, with twenty or so singers, all women and mostly younger than Dinah. At the first rehearsal, it took a while for Dinah to find her voice. She was rusty, and it was harder to read the score than it used to be. She croaked through a multitude of mistakes. But after they had warmed up, Dinah began to forget about her own voice, and to listen, instead, to the music the choir made. They sight-read Eleanor Daley's "Canticle to the Spirit." At first, Dinah thought it sentimental and too obviously religious, but there was something unexpected in the movement of the harmony, and it began to evoke in her a deep sense of yearning. Then, near the end, when their voices swelled together on the crescendo, Dinah experienced intense frisson. Tingling ran through her body like an electrical current, making her hair stand on end and her eyes prick with tears. She was so overcome, she nearly dropped her score and had to sit for a minute.

After rehearsal, Amanda coerced her into socializing over juice and cookies, but after ten minutes of supplying one-word answers about herself to various inquirers, she told Amanda they should go because she was tired.

Once she was alone in bed, however, all Dinah's tiredness left her. Her mind replayed the Daley song in an endless loop and ignited a ghost sensation of the tingling she had felt in rehearsal. She couldn't fall asleep until four in the morning. It was as if she had been shocked awake.

* * *

On Sundays, the choir sang during the service, and for the first time in her life, Dinah attended church regularly. She had been to various denominations of churches before, for funerals and weddings, sometimes at Easter or Christmas, but her parents had not been churchgoers. They had not, in fact, done anything as a family – even sharing dinnertime was a rare occurrence. Dinah's father was a banker and perpetually distracted by his work, and her mother barely left her bedroom. From a young age, Dinah avoided them both so she could pretend they were not avoiding her and each other, and they had lived together, yet singly, in a quiet house, enlivened only by the piano when she played it.

Dinah listened politely to the minister – a holder of two PhDs, who was both thoughtful and amusing, gentle yet intellectually rigorous. He didn't suggest there were any easy answers – except one: God was love. This confounded Dinah. How could it be so? There was so much worldly suffering. Surely love alone was not enough to fix things. Life was so much more complicated than that. Love was a grand idea, but it did nothing useful.

The afternoon after the minister had discussed the book of Job, Dinah knocked furiously on Amanda's front door. "It's impossible. How is it right? He can't just explain that away."

"Job? Yes, well, lots of people have trouble with that one, not surprisingly. Come on in."

Amanda's house was a jumble of books and ornaments and cats of various colours and sizes. On the wall where the TV might have gone if she had had one was displayed an extensive collection of old and recent family photos. Dinah found the disorder of Amanda's house oddly comforting when she would never have put up with it in her own house. She settled back against a thick down cushion and breathed deeply while she waited for Amanda to make tea.

Dinah tried to remember when she had last been in another person's home like this. There had been dinner parties with Alan's colleagues, and a long time ago, she had accompanied Michael to birthday parties. One woman had invited her to join a group of mothers for weekly coffee when Michael was eight or nine, but Dinah declined. She didn't like the immediate intimacy that was expected by other women because it would force her to reveal her awkward intensity. She remained insular and private; otherwise, they would see: she could not calibrate. When she had to, she engaged in the bland conversation that made her utterly forgettable, but nothing more than that. She had only managed to find herself with Alan because he had had a similar upbringing and had admired her circumspection, at first, and as a young woman, she had been attractive enough to make him look good, but not so beautiful that she might outshine him. When she was young, he declared proudly to her and others that she was "handsome."

Amanda handed Dinah a mug of tea. "Getting under your skin, is it?"

"How does any of this make sense to you?" Dinah's earlier agitation reappeared. "I feel like an utter fraud singing all those God songs. You believe in God – explain it to me." Dinah didn't mean to sound hostile, but there it was; she couldn't help it. Next, Amanda would tell her to leave and ask her to stop coming to choir.

But Amanda was unperturbed by Dinah's rudeness. "Believe in God? I don't, but I wish I could. I suppose people just know it, or they don't. It's not very logical, is it? I should give you better arguments, I suppose. Philosophical ones! Explain why someone would believe such a thing. But I don't know, and I don't think it's anyone's job to convince you, even if they could. You should maybe ask yourself why it worries you so much, though. Oh! Forgot the cookies." Amanda jumped up and returned to the kitchen.

"Well, it doesn't worry me, not really," Dinah said to herself, and waved her hand, as if to push the idea away. But it wouldn't shift; it *did* worry her. She breathed deeply to still her heart, but it was as if the air ballooned inside her, making her weightless. The more she tried to calm herself, the more immaterial she felt, until she was certain she was about to float away. She gripped the arm of the sofa and willed herself to stay tethered to the earth.

By the time Amanda returned, Dinah sat solidly upright. She pointed to the photos. "Tell me about your family." Then the easy conversation that had been denied Dinah her whole life somehow, finally, found its way into her mouth. It was miraculous; suddenly she chatted like a friend, speaking perfectly in a new language she thought she had never learned.

That night, as Dinah recalled her conversation with Amanda, the shivers she had experienced while singing again ran through her body. The feeling set the tips of her fingers on fire, scorched the soles of her feet. It was almost painful, and yet, a kind of ecstasy. She didn't want it to stop.

"Are you sure about this? It seems rather late to start believing in God," Michael said when Dinah called to tell him that she was now a believer.

"It's not as if I'm going to go out evangelizing!"

"Are you sure they're not just looking for donations?"

"Don't be cynical," she said. Michael cleared his throat. "We're all part of it. Before, it was just me –"

"I was there, Mother. And Dad."

"I know."

"Do you?"

"What do you mean? I did well with you. Look how successful you are!"

"Successful." His voice was tight. He cleared his throat again. "I imagine you should go to the doctor, Mother."

"I feel perfectly all right. I'm just trying to tell you that I have to live differently now. I have a responsibility to others. God wants me –"

"Honestly, Mother. Please go to the doctor."

"But I feel wonderful."

Dinah stayed for some time at the after-choir social that week. She sought out the organizer of the social action committee and threw her hat in the ring. "Whatever you need, Margaret," Dinah said. "I've been lacking."

"You kept a house and brought up a child – who's now a judge, no less! You've done okay. How were you lacking?" Amanda's question was rhetorical, but it struck Dinah that she should be able to answer it. There was something she had missed, something she was supposed to do and didn't.

"I just haven't done enough," Dinah said finally.

"Enough what?"

"You don't have to do anything," Margaret said. "God loves us no matter what. You don't have to run around doing good works."

"But Amanda is always checking in on the neighbours and helping people."

"Not because of God, though," Amanda said.

"We can use your help, in any case." Margaret lightly patted Dinah's back.

No one had touched Dinah for years. For a moment, she thought she might cry and embarrass herself, and turned away to gather her things. But she noticed something then, a point of incipient pain where Margaret's hand had been, a blast of heat, as though a blowtorch had been aimed at her upper vertebrae from far away. Just for a second or two, then it was gone.

. . .

Over the next few weeks, Dinah solicited donations of soap and socks and formula, helped people navigate city bureaucracy as they struggled to find affordable places to live and served meals to the hungry from the church basement. She was doing what God expected of her, and for the first time in her life she not only felt worthy, she was truly happy.

"I'm a do-gooder now," she told Michael a few weeks later.

"How are you getting on though? Have you been forgetting things?"

"You think my desire to help other people is dementia?"

"I don't understand this sudden change. You've never exactly been altruistic."

"I know I wasn't perfect, but I did the best I could."

"But you seem to be doing a better best now. For strangers."

"You don't need to keep being angry with me forever. God forgives me."

"Oh, but you were never cold and withholding to God." There was silence. Then a sigh. "Yes, we're doing pretty well, Mom. Anne is settling into her new job. We won't be able to take time off together this year, but maybe next. Thanks for asking."

The dial tone rang in her ear.

She would make it up to Michael. God would teach her how to love him better, and then he would see the change for himself and love her in return.

By the end of the month, Dinah's commitment to social action remained strong, but her energy began to wane. She retired early and slept late, napped in the afternoon. Two weeks in a row, she was too tired to go to choir rehearsal. Though she never missed the Sunday service, Amanda had to nudge her to stand when it was their turn to sing, and Dinah often lost her place in the music. She was not used to the new activity, she reasoned. She had been lazy and selfish for too long.

The more tired she became, the more likely she was to be visited by the tingling sensation. It could be set off by the slightest thing: a breeze carrying a scent she remembered, lilacs say, or fresh bread; the sight of a toddler eating an ice cream with intense focus and pleasure; one of Amanda's cats purring on her knee; the liquid, golden quality of sunlight in the late afternoon. And music, always music.

She tried to explain it to Amanda. "It's pins and needles, sort of, but more like bubbles fizzing, as if I'm filled with soda."

"That's just the shivers," Amanda said.

"Yes, but it's more than that. When it happens, it feels like every atom in my body has come alive, and I'm overcome with – I know, it sounds ridiculous – with joy. Although, sadness too. It used to be only when I was singing. But now it happens all the time."

Amanda looked at Dinah closely. "Do you think you should go to the doctor?"

"That's what Michael says. He is persistently prosaic." Amanda, a good listener, laughed gently and waited. Dinah went on. "It doesn't feel like any kind of sickness. It feels like its exact opposite. A doctor isn't going to be any help at all." Dinah hesitated. "I think it's a manifestation."

"Of what?"

"God."

Amanda shook her head slowly. "I don't know. If there was a God, I don't think he would really work like that."

"How do you know how He works? You don't really know

any more about it than I do. You don't even believe in Him. Why wouldn't He visit me?"

"I suppose." Amanda looked skeptical, but not offended by Dinah's outburst. "I still think it might be worth an MRI or something like that."

Dinah sighed deeply, annoyed with Amanda's inability to recognize the truth. "It's not physical!"

"I'm worried about you. You seem to be in some kind of emotional transition right now. Perhaps a hug would help."

"If you wish." Dinah leaned rigidly against Amanda's soft torso, and Amanda wrapped her arms gently around Dinah's back.

"Ah!" Dinah jumped as if she had just been stung. "I thought that had gone." There was no mistaking it this time, a flare of white-hot pain in her spine.

Later that month, Dinah sat on a straight-backed chair in the oncologist's consultation room and clutched her handbag against her chest while the oncologist delivered her verdict: Dinah had a malignant tumour at the bottom of her right lung, against her spine. As it grew it would exert increasing pressure on her nerves and spinal column. It was inoperable.

Dinah shook her head emphatically. "I don't smoke. I've never smoked. You've made a mistake."

"It's extremely rare, but it happens." The oncologist tipped her head to one side. "It can be genetic. Was there lung cancer in your family?"

But Dinah had never met and knew nothing about her extended family. She knew little about her own parents. After Dinah had left for university, her mother and father had gone their separate ways for good. Her father had moved with no forwarding address, and her mother had died soon after, though not from cancer.

"A Kleenex?"

Dinah hadn't realized she was crying. "But why now?" she said. "I've just . . . it doesn't make sense."

"I didn't think you would still be here," Dinah said to Amanda when she found her in the waiting room, not reading or staring at a phone, just sitting.

"Why would I leave?"

"Well, I've got six weeks of radiation, five days a week."

"God. That sounds difficult. I'll get the choir to help. We'll take turns," Amanda said. "Michael will come, won't he? Help you out."

"We don't have that sort of relationship."

"What sort is that?"

"We're not close."

"I'm sure he'll come."

Michael was even busier than usual, he told her; it was just that time of year. "And anyway," he insisted, "there would be no point of my coming until your treatment is finished. I can come when you're better. I have vacation time booked then."

"What if I'm not better?"

"I'll send you some money for cab fare so you can get to your appointments."

"I don't have to go on the weekends. You could come on Friday night and stay until Sunday."

"I expect you'll want to sleep then. I'll just be sitting around in your house. What would be the point?"

"I haven't seen you since your father's funeral."

"I did invite you to visit," he said. "You wouldn't come."

"Your wife doesn't like me."

"I can't come now. Anne's new job is demanding. And the children . . . we're busy, Mother. I have responsibilities."

"How are the children?" She could not recall their names, their ages. There were two, she remembered. She had never met them. "They could come with you."

"You're not making any sense." He spoke rapidly, impatient to hang up. "I'll come when your treatment is over."

"That would be nice. I know I am not good at showing it –" Dinah said.

"I'm sure you'll be fine. Don't you have God to help you?"

"I do love you, Michael."

She had never told him so before, but he had already hung up.

Amanda drove Dinah to her first appointment. Then, after some paperwork, Dinah left Amanda in the waiting room and went away to change into an open-backed gown. She padded in socked feet behind the nurse down the long, shiny corridor to the radiation room.

Dinah had already been tattooed and fitted for the bolster that would immobilize her when the ray was turned on. She lay face up on the cantilevered platform with her arms above her head, her gown pushed to her waist and her breasts exposed. She had expected to feel self-conscious about her near nakedness, but instead, she felt light and free. The room was a cool and calming non-place, and as the platform lifted her to be within the scope of the machine that would spiral around her to deliver the radioactive rays, Dinah had the almost pleasant sensation that she was floating in the air. It was medicine, but also something magical was happening.

But soon, as she lay with her arms up, the pain began to intensify. She wanted to sit up and release the pressure but knew she could not. Dinah had been told she wouldn't feel a thing, except for some discomfort on her skin, eventually. No one had warned her about the fire in her spine.

"Excuse me?" Her voice was flat and small in the empty room. "It burns." The claw-shaped machine spun slowly around her body.

Dinah squeezed her eyes shut and prayed to bear her suffering.

As soon as she was able to sit, she felt better immediately. "God must have known I was going to be in terrible pain," she said to the nurse who helped her down off the table. "I think that's why he found me because I couldn't have got through that without Him."

"It shouldn't hurt." The nurse looked startled.

"It was burning," Dinah said. "A terrible, terrible burning."

The doctor determined the position Dinah had to take for the radiation put pressure on the tumour where it bulged against her spinal column. "The nurse said you prayed your way through the first session, but I think morphine might be more effective." He handed her a bottle. "Take it twenty minutes before you get here. Every time."

As the treatments continued, Dinah gradually increased her dose of morphine until, by the fourth week, she swigged it straight from the bottle in the morning and again on the way to the hospital. Even then, the pain outstripped the morphine, and every time she lay on the bolster, the machine orbiting her thinning body, the burning came, and then, afterward, the spot remained, a cooling ember, until the next dose of painkiller at bedtime.

By the fifth week of treatment, Dinah slept all afternoon and most of the weekend, only getting up on Sunday morning for church. Though she had trouble focusing on the sermon, she enjoyed listening to the choir. When their voices echoed around the high ceiling, Dinah was soothed by the now-familiar tingling feeling, and she smiled because she knew that God was with her.

At first, Dinah assured herself that Michael would come and looked forward to his arrival patiently, but as she became more fatigued and confused, even his calls became less frequent. He would ask her how she was but offered only distracted "hmms" and "ahhs" when she told him about her ongoing and painful ordeal. She didn't tell him how afraid she was, she couldn't, but after a few weeks, she could hear herself whining, desperate for him to come. She had never asked Michael for anything before, and he had not asked her. That was how their relationship worked. But things were different now, surely he could see that.

"It's not just me, Mother. I can't just do whatever I want and leave my family."

"I'm your family."

"When have we ever been a family?" Michael said. "Even before you packed me off to boarding school, you ignored me."

"I did my best. Things were different in those days."

"I just can't come right now."

"It's very immature to punish me this way," Dinah snapped and slammed down the phone.

She comforted herself with anger after that and wouldn't call him back when he left messages. "He wishes I was already dead," Dinah sniffed to Amanda on the way to the hospital. Spring had fully taken hold of the city. Spindly, grey trees were showing their first buds, but dirt and garbage, until now covered by thick snow, littered the streets near St. Joseph's Hospital. "You would think he could forgive me. But no. He must punish me even now."

Amanda called him a coward, but made excuses for him, something about his inability to deal with his own anxiety about sickness and death. "You're punishing him too."

"Look at what I've done at the church, on the committee. Look at what I've gone through. Surely, I deserve better." But she wasn't sure. What did she deserve?

Dinah closed her eyes. Spring was an ugly season.

. . .

The treatment ended. Dinah was raw and burned where the radiation had done its work, not only on her back, but in her esophagus too. Because of the damage to her throat, it was painful to eat, and she became even thinner and frailer, until it was hard for her to even get out of bed. Amanda brought soup and sat with her while the liquid dribbled down her chin, and every few days she helped Dinah to lower herself into a warm bath. As Dinah sank into the water, she noticed the familiar tingling, but over the week it diminished, bit by bit, until it became nothing more than a low buzz just under her skin for only a few seconds, then nothing, until not even music could evoke the sensation. She wasn't sure, once it was gone, what it had meant, or if it had ever meant anything.

On Saturday night, Dinah finally answered Michael's call. He told her Anne had breast cancer. That was why he had been so distracted. Now they knew for sure, he couldn't leave Anne or the children. He began to cry on the other end of the line.

"I'm sorry," Dinah said. "That's terrible. How bad is it? What will happen next?"

"Do you honestly care?"

"Of course I do. I know what it's like. I –"

"It's always about you."

"That's not what I mean."

Michael was silent for a few seconds. "I know. I'm sorry I can't be there."

"I'm sorry too." She hung up.

The words felt so strange. It was as if someone had whispered in her ear, telling her what to say: I'm sorry.

Was there something else? She listened hard, but that was all.

. . .

The next morning, Dinah dressed awkwardly, then called Amanda and asked if she would take her to church. On the short drive, Dinah croakily assured Amanda she felt better. "I know the radiation worked," she insisted. "No more cancer. You'll see."

Amanda walked Dinah into the empty sanctuary. Dinah was much taller than Amanda, but now she felt insubstantial beside her. When she walked, it was as if her feet made no pressure on the ground. "I'm barely held together. I could fly away in an instant."

"You've lost a lot of weight." Amanda helped Dinah into the front pew.

"That's not what I mean."

"Right, I'll see you after the service. Got to get my gown on and do the warm-up. Just sit tight." Amanda patted Dinah's hand and left.

The church was Gothic-style, dimly lit, with a magnificently high roof and stained-glass windows all around. Above the chancel where the choir sat during the service, the window told the story of Revelation in crimson, bright blue and yellow: a fiery sun and stars falling from the sky, a city destroyed in the distance, a rainbow arched over it. Faceless figures were either cast below the earth or they sprouted wings and flew upward. Dinah wondered if the image was supposed to spark fear or elation.

The morning sun poured through the window and spilt the window's colours across the floor and over the cloth-covered altar, which had been already prepared for Communion with a jug and chalice and basket of bread.

Dinah had been embarrassed at first and awkward when she took Communion, but when she dipped the bread into the wine and put it in her mouth, in an instant it didn't matter: she had felt the joyous rush of God in her body – and every time after that. But it had been weeks since she had taken Communion.

Dinah lifted herself from the pew and came slowly to the altar. A muffled hymn from the rehearsing choir seeped through the walls. She steadied herself, then lit one of the candles. Its flame wavered and sent a thin trail of grey smoke snaking upward. Dinah lifted the jug with both hands. It was much heavier than she had expected, and her hands shook as she poured a teaspoon of wine into the cup. She took a piece of bread and dipped it in the liquid, placed the bread in her mouth and swallowed. Clouds outside dulled the window and washed the colours from the cloth. Dinah shivered, but it was only the cool air. She waited for the feeling to enter her.

"I thought so," she said aloud, finally. "Nothing. All this time." She was gullible, like Michael had said. God was just a fantasy she had used to make herself feel better about being utterly alone.

Dinah stared at her stick-thin wrists, the gauzy skin on the back of her hands, then down at her body, a grey sliver, barely extant. She imagined herself dissolving and joining the dim light and dust, atom by atom. She put her palm in front of her lips, breathed out slowly and felt her own warm, moist breath leave her body.

The choir's singing became louder, and the pain in her spine flared. She staggered, then fell, her knees thudding on the hard, wooden floor. A jolt shot up her spine and met the burning between her shoulder blades.

She gasped and reached out to steady herself, but before she could find purchase, she was yanked upward as if a great hand had hooked around her heart and lifted her from the ground. She hurtled toward the vaulted ceiling in a rush of air. Terrified, Dinah tried to scream, certain she would be dashed to pieces, but there was only a weak and desperate whimper from her raw throat.

She stopped short of the ceiling in a burst of light.

Then she understood: God was love. But not only love. God was fear too, and pain, and anger, and sickness. Love was suffering. There was no distinction. It was all one.

Dinah's mouth fell open, and her eyes fluttered and closed. Her chest expanded. She let go of the pain. Let go of her guilt and all her wanting. Let go of God. Everything was what it was supposed to be.

The pain in her back ignited and its white-hot light consumed her from within. She rose farther, and there was no ceiling, no world below. She drifted higher, weightless, a thin trail of smoke curling farther upward, fading, dissolving, until she was everywhere and everything at once.

ACKNOWLEDGEMENTS

So many thanks to the professors and students in the UBC optional-residency MFA program who provided invaluable feedback to me as many of these stories were written and all of them rewritten. Most special thanks to John Vigna who helped me make sense of the collection and pushed me hard to keep thinking about what these stories were and what they meant. Thank you to fellow graduate Karen Palmer for opening her home to me to visit and write and talk about writing. It would not have been possible to attend the program without financial support from the Humber College Union scholarship; I am extremely grateful.

Thank you, everyone at Wolsak & Wynn, for so kindly shepherding me through the publication process – Paul Vermeersch who took a chance on the work, especially, and Jen Hale for editing the book whole, but also, of course, Noelle Allen, Ashley Hisson, Jamila Allidina, for all you do. Jen Rawlinson – thanks for that cover!

I cannot thank enough my beautiful friend and poet Meaghan Strimas for reading this manuscript early and again, and for helping me through the agonizing process of finding a publisher. I would not have even begun to try to publish if it were not for Rachel Letofsky – thank you for believing in the manuscript when I didn't. Thank you to Nathan Whitlock, Gary Barwin and Amy Jones for your endorsements – it means a lot to be supported by other writers for whom time is so precious.

Chris, your love and faith in me allowed me to feel safe enough to write it all down; without you, this book wouldn't exist. Audie and Sam, you make me happy every day.

Love and thanks always to Joanna, my sister, sometimes mother and biggest fan. Where would I be without you?

Nicola Winstanley is a writer for adults and children. She has been shortlisted for the Governor General's Literary Award and is the recipient of the Alvin A. Lee Award for Published Creative Non-Fiction. Nicola's fiction, poetry and comix have been published in the *Windsor Review*, *Geist*, the *Dalhousie Review*, *Grain* magazine, *untethered* magazine and *Hamilton Arts and Letters*, among others. She holds an MA from the University of Auckland, NZ, and an MFA from UBC. Nicola works at Humber College in Toronto and lives in Hamilton, Ontario.